Boys, Beauty & Betrayal

ℬ℃ℬ

JC Conrad-Ellis

©2008
Nightengale Press
A Nightengale Media LLC Company

BOYS, BEAUTY & BETRAYAL

Copyright ©2008 by JC Conrad-Ellis
Cover Design ©2008 by Nightengale Press

For information about Nightengale Press please
visit our website at www.nightengalepress.com.
Email: publisher@nightengalepress.biz
or send a letter to:
Nightengale Press
10936 N. Port Washington Road. Suite 206
Mequon, WI 53092

Library of Congress Cataloging-in-Publication Data
Copyright Registeration: TXu1-332-359

Conrad-Ellis, JC,
BOYS, BEAUTY & BETRAYAL/ JC Conrad-Ellis
ISBN:1-933449-60-8
ISBN 13: 978-1933449-60-9
Teen Fiction

Copyright Registered: 2008
First Published by Nightengale Press in the USA
September 2008

10 9 8 7 6 5 4 3 2 1

Printed in the USA and the UK

This book is dedicated to the mighty men in my family:

Brian W. Ellis,
Thank you for being my mate, my buddy, my hero,
My babies' daddy, and my best friend. I love you! y.w.m.o.e.

Newby/Brian, Jr.,
You are my favorite only son. Strive to treat the women
in your life like your dad treats me or better! Newby, 6-10!

To my awesome brothers, John Conrad,
Kenneth Conrad & Robert Conrad,
My life was richer and better because you shared it with me!
Pickle juice and grits-n- gravy.
P.S. to Opie- Thanks for your encouragement
and nurturing throughout this project!

Kenny Conrad, Jr., Christopher Conrad & Ray Conrad –
The world's most fantastic nephews!
You make me proud, just by being you! Aunt Ginger

Bertrand W. Ellis,
Thank you for treating me like a daughter
and for raising such an awesome son.

George Conrad, David Conrad, Michael Conrad,
Nathan Andrews, Reginald Bishop, John H. Moore, III,
Marcelluls Stamps, Jr., Robert Jenkins –
Thank you for your uncle love and kindness!

Michael Williams, George Conrad, MD,
Robert Jenkins, Jr., Earl (Trey) Cole, III
Thank you for being extraordinary cousins!

Michael Coburn – MC,
You've always been like a brother to me, keep doing you! jc

In memory of my phenomenal cousin,
John Henry Moore, IV
(December 28, 1964 – June 3, 2007)
You will live on in our family forever!

GRATITUDE & ACKNOWLEDGEMENTS

First and foremost, I'd like to thank God for using me as the vessel to tell this story. It was God who blessed me with the gift of story telling, creative writing, and an ability to recall and recycle seemingly useless and minute details coupled with an overactive imagination that links it all together. And it was nothing but God that awakened me countless times in the wee hours of the morning where I could do nothing but pray and write. Thank you for enabling me to bloom where I was planted.

To my daughters, Bailey & Blair: Remember to seek wise counsel from the brave, smart, God fearing women that God will place in your life to help mentor and guide you on your journey. I pray that I am providing you with a foundation that will strengthen and enrich you while giving you the confidence to know that you too can be mothered by many women at different points in your life. May you always find unconditional love, joy, support and nurturing near the tree that is me. I will love you for always and like you forever! Boop, thanks for the title tips. Do you! Shadow, thanks for the dance breaks! Love, Mom

I humbly acknowledge and thank the quilt of wonderful women in my life (past and present) that helped me become that which I am. I will be eternally grateful for the mothering, friendship and love that they showed me. Somewhere on my journey, they touched and inspired me in a positive way and made it possible for me to birth this project. To these women: Please keep mentoring me and blessing me with your love, friendship, sunshine and shade, as I remain a humble work in progress. My life was made better by something that you unknowingly did or said, or simply because you were in it for a season, and for that I thank you. You are the roots of my tree!

Ernestine Conrad, Lillie Conrad, Amelia Bishop, Barbara Moore, Carolyn Conrad, MaryJane Stamps, Portia Conrad-LePage, Hilary Conrad, Lillian Marshall, Norma Jenkins, Arlene Cole, Anjanette Andrews, Jenelle Ellis, Necole Merritt, Yvonne Perry VanLowe, Helen

Jordan Cornet, Yvonne Manns, Andrea Conrad Parker, Sharon Ruff, Carla Namboodiri, Angie Chatman, Kelly West, Lisa Moore, Marsha White, Kay Virgil, Marlo Jenkins, Kyra Williams, Nikki Cole, Sonja Conrad, Madison Moore, Isis Ruff, Courtney Williams, Lori West, Tiffany Conrad, Lauren Williams, Angela Hall, Pam Gibbs, Gloria Collaso, Wendy Washington, Lisa Harston-LeDoux, Sylvia Stein, Sharon Dudley-Parham, Dominique Jacob Smith, Sherita Jackson Henderson, Deona Lewis Thomas, Kim Neely DuBuclet, Tamara Markey, Spring Capers, Kim Evans Rudd, Sheila Jackson, Rita Ellis, Rachel Rooney, Jennifer Weinert, Michelle Richardson, Joy Rooker-McLaurin, Jillonda Reed Washington, LaVerne Weatherly, Monica Chambers, Pam Foster, Zanette Sanders, Latoria Carroll, Estella Reid, Miriam Gonzales, Susan Dawkins, Rev. Wanda Washington, Donna Young, Maggie Ellis, Bonnie Danick, Rhonda Ellis, Alfreida Ellison, Jeanette Burrell, Shari O'Bryant, Kathy Witt, Eileen Suarez, Tanisha Turner, Tia Conrad, Heidi Barker, Veronica Hancock, Robin Rone, Cecelia "CeCe" Conrad, Lori Hayes Shaw, Charesse "Reesi" Foye, Eleanor Conrad, E. Kaye Wilson, Joyce Thomas, Donna Brumsfield, Phyllis Luster, Evelyn Owens, Terri Reisig, Dena Dodd Perry, Marsha Taylor, Renee O'Bryant, Sharon Lovett Solomon, Yolanda Durfield, Barbara Smith, Elaine Hampton, Barbara Barksdale, Monica Whitaker, Heidi Hickman, Ernestine Evans, Nicole Roberts Jones, Taylor Thomas, Gloria Materre, Janet Lucas, Chevez Wells, Tina Turner, Elaine Whitaker, Jacque Moore Bowles, Pat Wells, Paula Burris, Michelle Speller-Thurman, Kay Gustin, Karyn Roelke, Joan Drout, Kelly Gritzmacher, Tonya Nienhaus, Joyce Feaster, Juliet Webb, Jamie Allen, Alfreda Bradley-Coar, my publisher Valerie Connelly & the team at Nightengale Press, The Women of Delta Sigma Theta Sorority, Inc.: Chicago Alumnae Chapter, Milwaukee Alumnae Chapter, Theta Alpha Chapter, Northwestern University Alumnae Association, The mothers of Jack and Jill of America, Inc., Milwaukee Chapter & The Bible Study Ladies of Bristlecone Pines.

To my readers: I pray that you are being nurtured and mentored by a village of girls and women who will strengthen, challenge and encourage you to be your best self, and live your life on purpose each and every day! Never be afraid to be mothered and nurtured by all of the women who positively impact your life even if their time in your life is but a brief season. Their inclusion in your story is not by accident. Learn from them, treasure these encounters, embrace the wise counsel that is shared with you, and remember to always enter by the narrow gate.

Lastly, as the Alpha and the Omega, I thank God once again for my many blessings, for sustaining me always, for allowing his son, Jesus to die on a cross so that my sins would be forgiven, and for using me as the vessel to pen this tale for girls everywhere to read and enjoy.

CONTENTS

In loving memory of my father,
John Theodore Conrad, Sr.
(July 30, 1944–May 17, 2003)
I love you and miss you, Daddy!

*"Enter by the narrow gate; for the gate is wide, and the way is easy,
That leads to destruction, and those who enter by it are many.
For the gate is narrow and the way is hard, that leads to life,
And those who find it are few." Matthew 7:13-14
(The New Oxford Annotated Bible - Revised Standard Version)*

Chapter 1

Chapped Lips

The list complete, Tanisha chewed on the end of her pencil, her head already in a spin. She squeezed the empty metal tip that once held the eraser between her molars, pressing it firmly together like an empty tube of toothpaste. She winced as the metal tip touched another loose filling in the back of her mouth. Her tongue went on a recovery mission to massage and caress the wounded tooth. She rattled the pencil on the linoleum kitchen table with her thumb and bit her bottom lip as she studied her grocery list.

A natural list maker, she'd scribbled the menu and shopping list for her 14th birthday party months ago. A four foot sub sandwich would be the main food item complete with chips and soda. In her head, she planned that each guest would eat approximately four inches of the sub sandwich.

She studied her list and checked off all of the birthday party supplies that she'd lined up on the kitchen table: potato chips, Doritos, sweet dill pickles, grape and orange soda, red Hawaiian Punch and diet 7-UP. Tanisha was prepared to share the submarine sandwich with her three brothers and just prayed that there would be enough food for all of her guests. She imagined what her friends would say if she ran out of food.

"Tanisha ran out of food at her slumber party! Can you believe it? I've never been to a sleepover where they ran out of food! How tacky!"

Tanisha wanted her sleepover to be a hit. She'd used her babysitting money plus the Christmas money that she'd gotten from her great Aunt Lyn and her Grandmother Bootsy to buy the sandwich, chips and soda. Tanisha hated the word pop, even at fourteen.

Shortly after her family moved to Newberry East from Chicago, when Tanisha was ten years old, she was given a lesson in soda pop etiquette from a teenage sales clerk at the grocery store.

"Pop?" The clerk looked up from her shelving duties and slanted her eyes at Tanisha before responding.

"Can you tell me where the pop is?" Tanisha repeated her request louder this time.

The teenager's jaws moved left and right chewing on a large, pink wad of bubble gum. The clerk glared at Tanisha and twirled her stringy blonde hair. "It's soda pop, or soda for short. But it's not pop, you stupid kid! Only Chicago people call soda "pop" and my mother said that calling soda "pop" is ghetto and common! The soda is in aisle 13!" the clerk growled.

Tanisha didn't quite know what it meant to be common, but she'd watched enough episodes of *Good Times* and knew what ghetto meant, so soda it became.

The bottle of diet 7-Up looked out of place next to the bright red punch. She'd not planned to buy diet 7-Up, but Maria had personally requested it and she didn't want to disappoint her friend, so she picked up the smallest bottle that she could find.

She folded her list and stuffed it in her small disco pouch, grinning widely as she arranged the food on the metal card table that she'd placed in the dining room. She'd even bought generic paper plates, napkins and plastic silverware but Tanisha was careful to throw away the generic black and white paper wrapping before the guests arrived. She'd not had enough money to buy a tablecloth so she covered the metal card table with a white sheet.

She recounted the money in her disco pouch and confirmed that with tax and tip she would have just enough to treat her sleepover guests to the $2.99 pancake special at Golden Bear restaurant. No one had done that before. At other sleepovers, the moms usually cooked breakfast, but no one had taken the sleepover to a restaurant!

Tanisha inhaled deeply and wrinkled her nose. She quickly sprayed Glade air freshener around the room to try to mask the smoke and musk smell that hung in the air like a thick fog. She'd vacuumed with Carpet Fresh and had used Pine Sol to clean the bathrooms and kitchen floor, but the townhouse still contained an odor that Tanisha found distasteful. She sprayed the sofa and buried her face in one of the pillows and inhaled again. Satisfied that the offensive smell was masked, she plopped down on the sofa and opened the draperies to gaze out the window and await her guests.

Since nightfall, three inches of snow had already accumulated on the wooden railing adjacent to the living room window. Tanisha bit her lower lip and glanced at her watch confirming that it was now eight minutes past seven o'clock. It was December, and the weatherman had predicted a blizzard.

"It figures. It always snows on my birthday!" Tanisha groaned loudly.

But this year, the night's forecast called for record breaking cold and snow! Tanisha lived in Newberry East, Illinois, a suburb of Chicago. Newberry East was a small city surrounded by corn fields and open plains, so the area usually got snow drifts that were over four feet tall.

A moment of panic ensued for Tanisha. *What if no one comes to my party? Their parents aren't going to bring them out in this storm! This party has to be fun or I'll be the laughing stock of the eighth grade!* She closed her eyes and placed her hands in the praying position. *God! Please make it stop snowing! Or if you can't make it stop snowing, please get all of my friends here safely.* She glanced out the window and scowled. The snow was now coming down in large clumps.

She wanted her birthday slumber party to be a hit for her new friends. Her social standing depended on this party being a hit. Her family's move from Chicago's south side to Newberry East in third grade almost devastated her. She understood that her dad needed to be closer to his new job in Indiana, but she hated her new environment.

Tanisha Carlson had transferred to Mahala Elementary School in Newberry East for 3rd through 6th grade where there was only one other black girl in her grade. Her name was Dawn Brown. Dawn struggled with her studies and wore glasses the size of coffee mugs. She also carried a large tub of Vaseline intensive care petroleum jelly in her backpack and lathered the Vaseline on her full lips several times a day. In addition to her academic limitations, Dawn also lacked the coordination to jump Double Dutch or play four square at recess.

Tanisha usually tried to avoid Dawn on the playground. But often she found herself drawn to Dawn when the white girls at recess excluded her from their games, which was most days.

"Dawn, can't you jump rope? You're the only black girl that I know who can't jump Double Dutch," Tanisha stated firmly.

"I wear orthopedic inserts, and my mom says that they might get damaged if I jump around." Dawn's words bounced off the asphalt as she spoke with her head down.

"Well, do you want to play four square?" Tanisha was anxious to do something physical.

"The ball might hit my glasses, so I better not," Dawn said, reaching into her small pouch.

Tanisha glared at Dawn. *"Why do you keep smearing Vaseline on your lips? It looks like you've been sucking on a greasy chicken bone!"* Tanisha turned her head slightly and mumbled under her breath. *"This girl doesn't like to do anything that I like to do. I don't know why the teacher always assigns us to be partners in class."*

Dawn took a deep breath. *"Tanisha, I heard what you said,"* Dawn whispered softly. *"I have to put a lot of Vaseline on my lips because I have eczema and the Vaseline keeps my lips from getting chapped. And I think the teacher puts us together because we're the only two black girls in sixth grade,"* Dawn offered innocently as she dabbed in her Vaseline jar and applied another slathering on her already moist lips.

Tanisha looked up startled, not realizing that she'd spoken loud enough for Dawn to hear her. *"Oh. Well, I think you have enough Vaseline on your lips now,"* Tanisha replied.

Dawn's family moved to Texas the summer between sixth and seventh grade. Tanisha had been excited to transfer to Battle Creek Junior High School (BCJH) where she met other black students most of whom had attended Hickwood Elementary in Newberry East.

Tanisha's thoughts were interrupted by a car door slamming. She snapped out of her daydream and saw Maria and Lori climbing out of Maria's mom's new Toyota Celica. She grinned widely as her eyes stared upward. *Maria Wesley made it to my party! Thanks, God! I owe you one!* Tanisha ran to the front door and opened it before they reached the sidewalk. She squeezed her lips together and shivered as the snowstorm blew bits of snow into the tiny foyer.

The most popular girl at Battle Creek Junior High, Maria Wesley had long naturally straight hair that was feathered like Farrah Fawcett on *Charlie's Angels.* Her skin was a deep olive tone and she was often mistaken for Mexican or Puerto Rican, especially at Chi Chi's restaurant where most of the wait staff was Latino. Maria was a clothes horse who had all of the latest designer jeans and corduroys: Calvin Klein, Jordache and Gloria Vanderbilt. Maria and Tanisha were in four classes together so Tanisha was treated to a daily fashion show with Maria's designer jeans.

17

Tanisha was so glad to see them that she didn't care that Maria had on yet another new pair of Calvin Klein jeans. As she shivered in the doorway, Tanisha glanced down at her well worn Calvin Kleins and hoped that her friends wouldn't notice that she'd worn them three times last week at school.

At five feet seven inches, Tanisha was considered tall for her age. She had narrow hips that stretched down to long muscular legs. Tanisha was pleased with her body's development except for her flat chest. Her friends all had small buds and were beginning to fill out their training bras. Tanisha wore a training bra, but her buds were the size of small dimes as opposed to the small lemons of her friends. She gave herself a tight squeeze before rubbing her hands together for warmth.

Maria and Lori giggled up the walkway carrying their sleeping bags and overnight duffels. Lori Perkins was petite with short black hair that she wore cropped at her neck. Her eyes were chestnut brown and looked exotic against her dark brown skin. Lori was curvy in all the right places. Like Tanisha, Lori was also one of four siblings, but had two brothers and one sister to Tanisha's three brothers. Lori was in Humanities class with Tanisha, Maria and Rashanda but wasn't in the honors math and science classes. Tanisha and Lori had become fast friends.

Before Lori and Maria made it to the door, a green Lincoln pulled in front of the house and Rashanda, Justine and Grace hopped out.

Rashanda Jordan was in all of the same classes as Tanisha and Maria and had transferred to Hickwood Elementary from a parochial school in Hyde Park, Illinois. Rashanda had a heart of gold but was going through an incredibly awkward stage with big round glasses and a mouth full of braces. She was rail thin and lacked the slightest hint of adolescent development. She wore her hair in pig tails with

18

bright colored pony tale holders that secured her short hair. It wasn't a good look. Rashanda reminded Tanisha of Dawn, except Rashanda was smart. *If you're going to be funny looking, you'd better at least be smart,* Tanisha thought whenever she looked at Rashanda.

Grace Dudley was not in any of Tanisha's honors classes but secured an invite to the slumber party because she was friends with Lori, and Lori had suggested that Tanisha invite Grace. Tanisha trusted that if Lori liked Grace then she should try to get to know Grace too. Grace was nice, but she and Tanisha hadn't really clicked yet. Grace was five feet ten inches tall and had long, strawberry blonde hair that carried a natural body wave and her eyes were the color of root beer. Her skin was golden brown as though she had a year round sun tan. Grace was self conscious about her height and walked with her shoulders hunched over in an effort to appear a few inches shorter than her five feet ten inch stature.

Justine Wellington and Grace were best buds so Tanisha invited Justine to round out the group. Justine was pudgy and jovial. She wore her hair pulled back in a single pony tail that bounced off of her shoulder blades. Justine had a warm smile and deep laugh. Like Tanisha, Justine had not attended Hickwood Elementary and had moved to Newberry East over the summer. Justine was always nice and Tanisha hoped to get to know her better to increase her circle of friends in middle school.

"Happy birthday, Tanisha! It's so cold outside!" Maria wiped the snow from her shoulders.

"Yeah, happy birthday, girl! I'm so glad my mom still let me come. I thought she was going to make me cancel since it's supposed to be a blizzard. Plus, since it is Friday the thirteenth she didn't want to leave the house. She's superstitious," Lori said.

"My mom is superstitious too, but my dad told her to get over herself and take us to the party," Rashanda said. She and the other girls stomped the snow from their boots and left them in the foyer to dry.

"I'm so glad that you guys were able to come to my party! I've never been superstitious about Friday the thirteenth, since my birthday falls on the thirteenth." Tanisha hung their coats in the hall closet praying that the wire hangers could support the heavy wet coats. She took their overnight bags and sleeping bags and stacked them in a corner of the living room.

"Tanisha, don't take my bag yet, I need to get something." Maria reached into her duffel bag and pulled out a small tub of Vaseline and smeared it on her lips.

"You kill me with that Vaseline. Why don't you just use chapstick or lip gloss?" Lori asked.

"I use both, but Vaseline works better. Don't knock it until you've tried it." Maria handed around the small tub of Vaseline and all of the girls smeared some on their lips.

Tanisha giggled as she put a liberal slathering of the petroleum jelly on her lips. *I crucified Dawn for using Vaseline and now I'm using it too!*

"What's so funny, Tanisha?" Grace rubbed her hands together and lightly shook the snowflakes from her long hair. "Where do you want us to put the presents?"

"Maria's Vaseline reminded me of something," Tanisha said, as she waved her hand across her face dismissively. "You can put the gifts in the corner with the sleeping bags," she replied as Strongest bounced down the stairs and boldly walked up to the girls, his snout working overtime as he investigated the girls' scents.

"I forgot that you had a dog. What's his name again?" Justine patted the pet's head lightly.

"His name is Strongest," she smirked. Tanisha held up her hand to silence the next question. "Don't ask. It's a dumb name, I know.

My mother named him that. Just don't ask," she pleaded.

"Well, I'm allergic to animals, and I hate dogs." Maria used Lori as a shield to hide from the small pet.

"He's really friendly, but I'll put him away if you're allergic," Tanisha offered.

Maria rolled her eyes at the black mongrel, who now sniffed the sleeping bags and pillows. "We'll see how it goes," Maria replied. "I took my allergy medicine, but if my eyes start watering, I'll let you know."

"I've never been to your house before. Can we see your room?" Justine asked.

Tanisha inhaled deeply. *Oh my God! I can't show them my room! It never occurred to me that they would want to see my room! We didn't see Rashanda's room at her slumber party. They know. What am I going to say when they ask me?* "Sure. I mean it's nothing to see really. It's pretty small. I'll take you guys upstairs later but first let's eat." *Maybe they'll forget about wanting to see my room.*

"Good idea. I'm starving," Rashanda said.

"You're always starving, you eat like a wrestler, but you only weigh eighty five pounds. You crack me up," Lori laughed.

The party was underway and the predicted blizzard was in full swing when Billie yelled downstairs.

"Tanisha, let Strongest out!"

"Okay!" Tanisha yelled back. *The sound of her voice makes me want to vomit sometimes.*

Instead of walking Strongest, the family just opened the door and he ran outside. Tanisha walked to the back of the town house and into the kitchen. Strongest instinctively followed her and quickly squeezed through her legs and ran out the back door into the yard.

The snow drift covered the three steps of the back porch cement stoop and the snow was coming down in heavy thick flakes. Strongest raced into the night and ran out of sight. He was tagged and collared, and the area was surrounded by woods so he never wandered too far from their house. Tanisha closed the back door and went back to the task of hosting her birthday party.

Tanisha's older brother Jack was at swing choir practice so he wasn't eating the submarine sandwich. Her youngest brother Allen didn't eat meat so he wasn't touching the sub, and her younger brother Byron had only had a small slice. So it looked like they'd have enough for everyone to have seconds if they wanted! *Whew! At least we're not going to run out of food! One crisis averted! Besides, the chips and cake can serve as filler food for munchies later.*

Tanisha was just beginning to relax and enjoy the party when Billie came down the stairs. Billie was dressed in bright orange polyester hot pants with bell bottom flares and a matching halter top with a short sleeve tee-shirt underneath. Billie also had on red Candies slides and her face was completely made up. Make-up? *Why does Billie have on make-up to help me host the party? And why is she dressed like that?* Tanisha prayed that her friends didn't notice the painted lady in the room.

Lori was the first to notice. "Hi, Mrs. Carlson. You look pretty."

"It's **Ms. Peterson**. Thank you, Maria," Billie replied. "I have a date," she giggled, snapping her fingers and swaying her hips. "You teenagers aren't the only ones who can still have a good time!"

"I'm, Lori," she corrected softly.

"That's right. Maria is the one with the long, good hair. Thank you, Lori," Billie finished.

Lori shook her head and fingered her short hair. Tanisha blushed crimson. *You're still married to my dad, you witch! Legally, your name is still Carlson!*

Her name was Billie Mae Peterson, and she was Tanisha's mother. Even though she had only been separated from Tanisha's dad for two months, she'd already started referring to herself using her maiden name – Peterson. Hearing Billie use her maiden name was the final straw, the last nail in the coffin that sealed all hopes of a marital reconciliation.

The separation had caught Tanisha and her brothers by surprise. Tanisha's parents often argued, but she never expected that one of their arguments would lead to divorce. Tanisha was still numb from the shock of her dad moving out when less than one week later, Billie began to accompany Aunt Shanay to the local singles hot spots. Their favorite place was the Dating Game lounge on Chicago's far south side.

I can't believe that she just insulted my friend, and she's going out tonight! My friends are going to think that my mother is a tramp! Tanisha was embarrassed beyond belief.

Tanisha enjoyed referring to Billie as She behind her back because Tanisha knew that it drove Billie crazy. One day Billie overheard Tanisha and her brothers referring to her in the third person and became outraged. "I'm not a dog, don't call me she," Billie barked. "Call me Mommy!" And from that moment forward, Tanisha referred to her mother as Billie or "She" behind her back.

Tanisha had to admit that she did look pretty. Billie was five feet two inches tall and weighed one hundred and fifteen pounds. When her hair was done and she had on make-up, she was striking. Besides, she was only thirty five years old and after four children she was still a petite size four.

Nonetheless, Tanisha wanted to die. She wanted to curl up in a corner, cry and die. Her mother was the only separated woman in the group. All of the other guests were from solid two parent households. It was bad enough that Tanisha lived in the wrong area and her parents had recently separated, but now instead of hosting the party, Billie was going out. Tanisha was humiliated.

Using the wall to brace herself, Billie slipped out of her Red Candies slides and pulled on her brown leather boots as Tanisha walked up to her.

As if on cue, the slumber party guests walked into the small dining room to get more food.

"I'm going out for a while," Billie repeated. "Call Aunt Shanay if you need anything while I'm gone," Billie stated.

"Don't forget that you have to take us to Golden Bear tomorrow morning for breakfast," Tanisha whispered.

Billie let out a frustrated sigh and fumbled in her purse pulling out a cigarette. She flicked a blue lighter and lit her cigarette letting it dangle between her lips as she buttoned her rabbit coat. "Why can't they have breakfast here?" She spoke through her lips with the cigarette perched expertly on the side of her mouth.

"We don't have enough breakfast food for everyone. We don't even have any milk left. Besides, I want to take everyone to Golden Bear with my birthday money from Grandma Bootsy," Tanisha whispered. She didn't want her friends to hear the birthday breakfast surprise and was glad that they had walked into the dining room to get snacks and change the music.

Billie shook her head at Tanisha and exhaled, blowing smoke in her daughter's face. "Fine! If that's how you want to spend your money, that's your choice. It's your money," Billie shrugged. Billie slung her purse on her shoulder and stepped into the drifting snow, gripping her red Candies slides against her chest.

Tanisha knew where she was headed. Lately, Billie had been spending a lot of time with a man known only as Ray. From eavesdropping on conversations between Billie and Aunt Shanay, Tanisha knew that Ray was twenty eight years old to Billie's thirty five. Billie had met him at the Dating Game. She'd never brought Ray around her children and he never called her at home. But recently, Billie had been driving to his place with a plate of food that she'd prepared. Tanisha didn't know Ray but had formulated an opinion about him. She thought he was pond scum.

Billie wrapped the thin rabbit fur around her shoulders and studied the blizzard. She turned around and placed a hand on the front door thinking that perhaps she should reconsider her decision to drive into the city in a blizzard. The wind whipped snow in her face pulling her cigarette from her lips and into the night. She walked swiftly to her car, started it up and wiped off the front and back windshields before carefully steering the car out of the parking lot.

Tanisha leaned against the door, determined not to cry. She inhaled deeply and tried to look on the bright side. *At least she won't be here to ruin my party. Good riddance!*

"Do you guys want to call boys now or later?" Tanisha asked.

"Later. Let's play I believe in Mary Worth," Maria said.

"What's Mary Worth?" Justine asked.

"Yippee! A Mary Worth Rookie!" Grace rubbed her hands together and leaned into Justine. "Here's how it goes. You go into a dark room that has a mirror and you turn out all the lights. Then you chant 'I believe in Mary Worth' ten times and you'll see the reflection of a woman in the mirror with snakes in her hair."

"Do you really believe that works?" Tanisha asked.

"I've never seen her, but I've heard that it works," Lori said

Rashanda chewed on her sandwich and swallowed. "You guys, I don't think that we should do that," she suggested. "It sounds kind of spooky. If you guys want to do it, go ahead, but I'm not going to do it. It's almost like devil worship."

"Lighten up, Rashanda. It's all in fun," Maria teased. "Besides, Lori is the church girl, and she's game to try it." Maria applied more Vaseline to her lips.

"Well, you guys go for it. I'm staying right here." Rashanda took another bite from her sandwich.

"Fine, suit yourself. We need a mirror. Where can we do it?" Maria stood up and stretched her arms to the ceiling.

"We can go in the powder room," Tanisha offered.

"That bathroom is too small for all of us to squeeze into. Don't you have a mirror in your room?" Maria asked.

"I have a mirror in my room." Tanisha shifted her weight and bit her lower lip.

"Perfect! Let's go to your room. Take us upstairs," Maria said.

Tanisha led the group up the stairs to the second floor. When she reached the top she quickly closed Billie's bedroom door. Her brothers were in their room watching a small black and white television and closed the door when they heard the girls approaching. Tanisha walked into her room. *Here we go.*

A small twin size bed was stationed against the window with a full size quilt covering the mattress. The over sized quilt draped the floor. The twin mattress sat on a metal frame with no box spring. The bed lacked a headboard and was pushed against the wall for support. Next to the bed was a small, three drawer, cardboard dresser that held Tanisha's underwear and socks. To the left of the dresser, a floor length mirror was propped against the wall.

"This room is so small," Justine whispered to Grace. "Are we all going to fit in here?"

"It's not that small," Grace replied. "My room isn't much larger than this."

Tanisha wanted to melt into the floor boards. Her heart dipped into her stomach, and she felt her hands begin to tremble.

She didn't want her friends to see the shame plastered across her face and was glad that the room was dark.

"What's that smell?" Lori wrinkled her nose.

"The people who lived here before us had a cat," Tanisha stammered. "And the cat stayed in this room," she lied.

"I know what you mean. We used to have a cat and he would sometimes pee on the edge of the carpets. Cat urine soaks through to the carpet padding and you can't get the smell out. We had to replace the carpet," Justine said.

"My parents, I mean my mother is working with the management company to get the carpet replaced in here." Tanisha prayed that no one tried to sit on her bed.

"We're wasting time, let's get started. Turn off the light," Maria said.

Tanisha reached into the closet and pulled the string to turn off the only light in the room.

The room became midnight black. The girls giggled in the darkness.

"Quiet everyone! Close your eyes but face the mirror!" Maria ordered.

"Where is the mirror? I can't see it," Justine said.

"Tanisha, turn on the light again," Maria sighed loudly.

Tanisha reached into the closet and waved her hand until she felt the pull cord. She pulled on the cord to turn on the light.

"The mirror is leaning against that cardboard dresser," Maria said.

"Let's hold hands so we can really conjure up her spirit," Lori suggested.

"Good idea. Everyone, face the mirror," Maria said. "Tanisha, turn off the light."

The girls held hands and faced the mirror.

"I believe in Mary Worth. I believe in Mary Worth." Maria's tone was serious as she repeated the phrase.

"Maria, are we supposed to say it with you?" Justine giggled.

"I don't remember. But I know that I have to say it ten times and each time someone interrupts me I have to start over." Maria cleared her throat.

"I believe in Mary Worth. I believe in Mary Worth. I believe in Mary Worth. I believe in Mary Worth. I believe in Mary Worth. I believe in Mary Worth. I believe in Mary Worth. I believe in Mary Worth. I believe in Mary Worth. I believe in Mary Worth." Maria squeezed Tanisha's hand firmly. "Open your eyes!"

The girls opened their eyes and saw darkness.

"This is so silly. Tanisha, please turn on the light. I'm going back downstairs," Justine groaned.

"Come on you guys, let's try it again," Maria pleaded.

"I'm going downstairs too," Grace said.

"You guys didn't believe! That's why it didn't work! This time let's say it in unison," Maria suggested.

"Let's go. I'm ready for some cake!" Tanisha was anxious to get her friends out of her room before someone discovered the secret in her mattress.

Chapter 2

Let It Snow

The next morning, the girls awoke starving as only fourteen year old girls can after a night of eating, dancing and giggling. Everyone was in a jovial mood and anxious to eat breakfast when Tanisha looked out the window. Over two feet of snow had fallen overnight.

The sun shone brightly and Tanisha squinted as she admired the winter wonderland. Children were already outside sledding down the hill in front of their townhouse.

Tanisha walked away from the window, but ran back and did a double take when she didn't see the family car, Bruce the Blue Goose. Bruce the Blue Goose was the nickname that Tanisha's brother Jack had given the family's electric blue Caprice Classic. He loved Batman and wanted to name the family car the Bat Mobile but decided that the large family car looked more like a lazy goose than the slick Bat Mobile so he settled on Bruce Wayne's first name and labeled the car Bruce the Blue Goose.

Where was Bruce? Maybe Jack took Bruce to go to the store to get Billie some cigarettes. Although Jack was only fifteen and only had his learning permit, Billie would sometimes allow Jack to take the car to run quick errands for her. Tanisha looked at the sidewalk and noticed that there were no footprints in the snow.

Tanisha raced upstairs and quietly opened Billie's bedroom door. Billie's bedroom was empty and although she never made her bed, Tanisha could tell that Billie hadn't slept in her bed that night.

Jack was asleep in his room. Her heart raced. It was clear that Billie hadn't come home last night.

She checked the refrigerator. There wasn't enough milk and cold cereal for all of the guests. Besides, that wouldn't go over very well with the guests who were expecting a hot breakfast. Tanisha hadn't thought to buy Aunt Jemima pancake mix and syrup as a back up plan since she knew that Billie wouldn't prepare breakfast for them. She never prepared breakfast for her family. And the family didn't have a pancake griddle and cooking pancakes in a skillet didn't produce the right shape and texture. Pancakes needed to be cooked on a griddle. Plus, Tanisha didn't have any surplus funds from her birthday money for a 'just in case Billie spends the night out' back up plan.

Tanisha's stomach churned and her thoughts raced. *After a sleepover, the moms always made a special hot breakfast: blueberry pancakes, French toast or something special. Rashanda's mom made waffles after her sleepover. Doesn't Billie know this? Isn't this rule in the mothering handbook? We have to get to Golden Bear!*

If she sent her friends home hungry, her 8th grade social standing would be destroyed. *If Billie ruins my sleepover, I will hate her forever!*

Seconds into her panic attack, the phone rang. It was Billie.

"I'm in the city. It was snowing too badly so I stayed at Ray's," Billie stated casually. Tanisha could hear her taking a pull from her cigarette. Billie's tone was calm and indifferent.

"Are you going to make it back to take us to Golden Bear?" Tanisha asked.

"Did you hear what I just said, Tanisha? I'm still in the city, and the car is covered with snow!" Billie whispered in a loud voice.

"Well, what are we supposed to do? There's nothing to eat here and everyone's hungry. We don't even have any milk for cereal. I can't send my friends home without breakfast." Tanisha could feel her eyes welling with tears.

There was a long silence. "I will get there when I can." The phone went dead. Billie had hung up.

The tears flowed freely. Although Tanisha didn't want to cry in front of her new friends, she couldn't help it. She told them of her special breakfast birthday plans and explained that her mom was stuck in the city due to the snowstorm. They all expressed sympathy and understanding and said that they would call their moms and push back their pick-up times. Rashanda offered to call her mom to pick up everyone and take the group to Golden Bear. Tanisha thanked her for the offer, but assured her that Billie would be back shortly. Besides, Tanisha didn't want to advertise to the other parents that her mother had spent the night away during her child's birthday party. They would find that out soon enough.

So the girls waited. They munched on birthday cake, chatted and waited. Two hours went by, and as the breakfast hour loomed closer to lunch, and everyone was preparing to call their rides, Billie drove up. She burst through the door and rolled her eyes at Tanisha. "I'll take you in fifteen minutes."

Aunt Shanay arrived at the same time as Billie and for once Tanisha was glad to see her. Tanisha thought that Aunt Shanay was a loser. She had gotten pregnant in high school and dropped out to have a baby. The baby's father joined the army and never returned. Aunt Shanay then married a short postal worker that she didn't love so that he could support her and her child but proceeded to cheat on him with any man who would buy her a beer. Aunt Shanay's presence motivated Tanisha to study harder in school. Tanisha despised Aunt Shanay, and feared that Billie was following in her sister's footsteps. But in all of Tanisha's careful party planning, she hadn't considered that the family car wasn't big enough to carry six teenage girls plus her two younger brothers. Billie was resigned to abandon the Golden Bear mission when Aunt Shanay offered to drive her car too.

The girls piled into the Blue Goose and Aunt Shanay's brown speckled Volkswagen beetle and headed to the Golden Bear restaurant. The roads were snow covered and icy, but they managed to make it without skidding into a ditch.

Once seated, Tanisha announced to her friends that everyone had to order the two dollar and ninety nine cent pancake special which included a small juice and choice of bacon or sausage.

"I don't want pancakes," said Grace. "I want an omelet."

"I'd rather have waffles," offered Maria.

"Can't we order what we want, Tanisha?" Lori asked innocently.

Uh oh! How could she explain to her friends that she was paying for breakfast (not her mother) and that she only had enough for everyone to order the breakfast special? Tanisha swallowed hard and took a deep breath.

"Let people order what they want, Tanisha! Stop trying to control everything. It's too early for that," Billie stated firmly. Billie took a pull from her cigarette and continued whispering with Aunt Shanay.

Had she heard Billie correctly? Billie was letting people order what they wanted! Tanisha shrugged her shoulders and encouraged her friends to order.

The girls enjoyed their meal and grabbed their jackets, hats and gloves. It had started to snow again, and the temperature had dropped.

The girls went to the restroom to freshen up when Billie grabbed Tanisha's arm. "Tanisha, I need your money for breakfast." Tanisha reached inside her purse and quickly handed Billie the thirty three dollars in her disco pouch.

Billie counted the money. "Tanisha, this isn't enough. Is this all you have?" Tanisha stared silently at Billie shaking her head yes. She feared that Billie might explode, but there was nothing she could do. Tanisha didn't have any more money. She stared Billie squarely in the eye with a look that spoke volumes. *Now you see why I wanted everyone to order the pancake special, stupid!* She wished her mother could read her thoughts. Tanisha zipped her jacket and ran to catch up with her friends.

The girls piled into the cars dreading the afternoon of homework ahead of them.

"I think I left my scarf at the table," Maria said.

"I'll grab it for you." Tanisha ran inside the restaurant beaming with pride. By all standards, her slumber party had been a hit. Her friends were well fed and entertained and all were talking about how much fun they'd had. As she approached the table she overheard the waitress commenting to the busboy.

"This table ordered over fifty dollars worth of food and left a two dollar tip, can you believe that? A two dollar tip for a fifty dollar meal! Can't black people figure out percentages? Two dollars is not even ten percent! And I busted my butt serving them! I deserved at least a fifteen percent tip!" Frozen in her tracks with embarrassment, Tanisha considered slinking out of the restaurant. The waitress and busboy hadn't seen her. She pulled her shoulders back, took a deep breath and quietly walked up to the chair where Maria had been sitting. Ignoring the waitress' icy stares, Tanisha slowly pulled the orange scarf from the back of the chair and turned to leave. But something burned inside her and she turned around.

"I heard what you said," Tanisha shared softly. "And I'm sorry that my mother didn't leave you more of a tip. You were a nice waitress," she stammered. "I used my birthday money to pay for most of the bill," Tanisha explained staring into the waitress' face. "I'd give you more money for the tip if I had it, but I don't," she admitted. "And for the record," she continued confidently. "Black people can figure percentages. You deserved at least seven dollars and fifty cents as a tip," she finished. Her head lowered, she walked away before the stunned waitress could respond.

Rashanda's mom was waiting for them in front of the house when they got back from the restaurant. The girls ran into the townhouse, grabbed their things and piled into the car. Tanisha stood in the foyer stomping snow from her boots. Billie brushed past Tanisha and walked through the house without removing her coat or her boots, trailing snow footprints on the chocolate brown carpet. She opened the back door, and stared aimlessly at the snow. Her eyes scanned from left to right. "Strongest! Strongest!" she yelled into the snow. Billie spun around and asked no one in particular. "Did anyone let Strongest in last night?"

Chapter 3

John & Judy

It had been over seven days and Strongest was still missing. He was tagged and collared, but no one had called to say that they'd found him. Billie Mae feared the worst. She'd grown attached to the mutt and looked forward to his warm greeting each night when she came home. Whenever a car would pull in front of the townhouse, Strongest would immediately run to the window. Upon recognizing the Blue Goose, he would wag his tail and wave his head wildly in the window, racing to the door as the family ascended the stairs. Once in the foyer, Strongest would run in circles doing a doggie happy dance.

The night of Tanisha's birthday party, Billie's evening with Ray had not gone well. That morning, he'd broken off their relationship by telling her that he had decided to get back together with his ex-girlfriend. Billie was devastated. When she came home, she noticed that Strongest hadn't run to the window. Distracted by her wounded pride, she assumed that Tanisha's friends from the sleepover were playing with him. When they returned from Golden Bear and Strongest didn't run to the window, she became worried. Tanisha replayed the scene in her head.

"Strongest! Come here, boy!" Billie searched the snow for footprints. "Tanisha, come here! Last night, did you go to the back to see if he was waiting on the back porch?" Billie demanded.

"No. I let him out like you told me to," Tanisha said softly, her hands trembling with fear.

"But did you check to see if he was trying to get back in?" Billie asked firmly.

Tanisha didn't know what to say. She'd been so focused on her party that she'd never checked to see if Strongest was outside on the back porch. At night when they let him out, Billie or her brothers normally heard him scratching at the back door and would open it for him. With the music playing, and her friends giggling and partying, Tanisha hadn't thought about the dog.

"Answer me!" Billie shrieked.

"No. The music was kind of loud so I probably didn't hear him." Tanisha held her breath.

Billie stared at Tanisha for several seconds. Time seemed to stand still "I can't believe you. It's always about you. You had to have that damn party. And now my dog is probably dead in a snowdrift somewhere, and it's your fault!" Billie pointed her finger into Tanisha's chest.

Tanisha stared at Billie with a sad expression. Paralyzed by fear, she felt herself holding her breath. She forced herself to inhale slowly through her nostrils.

"I'm sorry. I'll go out and look for him," Tanisha offered.

"You're sorry all right. You're so sorry it makes me sick. It's too late now. With all the snow we got last night, he's probably buried alive in the back of the house. Don't bother looking for him now." She spat the words at Tanisha before slowly removing her finger from her daughter's chest. Billie closed the back door and brushed past Tanisha and down the small hallway.

Tanisha fought back tears. She didn't want to give Billie the satisfaction of watching her cry. From past experience, she knew that Billie's verbal cruelty only intensified whenever Tanisha cried.

Allen and Byron stood in the small dining room. "What happened to Strongest?" Byron asked.

"*Your sister killed him. That's what happened.*" Billie kicked off her boots, threw her coat on the sofa and stomped upstairs to her room.

"*Tanisha, what happened?*" Byron asked.

"*I just let him outside like we always do, but he didn't come back last night. He must have gotten lost in the snowstorm.*" The tears flowed freely down Tanisha's cheeks.

"*Don't cry, Tanisha. It wasn't your fault,*" Byron consoled.

"*Good. I was tired of walking that mutt every morning anyway. Don't sweat it, Tanisha.*" Allen patted Tanisha on the shoulder.

Tanisha wiped her face and grabbed her backpack to start her homework, plopping down on the sofa next to Allen as they watched television.

Tanisha snapped out of her daydream. She'd prayed for Strongest each night. As much as she hated Billie and the dumb name that she'd given the pet, she was attached to the little mongrel mutt. She dabbed her eyes and reapplied her eye liner. Still grieving, she wouldn't let Billie's words stain her plans. She shook her hair and wiggled into her Calvin Klein jeans. She knew that she had at least twenty minutes before Lori's mom picked her up to take them to the John & Judy teen mixer, and she wanted to make sure that she was ready when Mrs. Perkins arrived. She misted her neck and wrist with the new Love's Baby Soft cologne that she'd received as a birthday present from Grace and applied her strawberry lip gloss.

Tanisha was excited to be going to her first teen mixer with Maria, Lori and Rashanda. All week she'd been afraid that her friends' parents would forbid them from associating with her once they learned that Billie had not been home the night of the slumber party. Tanisha was so preoccupied with worry about how her friends would treat her on Monday that she was tempted to fake a stomach ache so she wouldn't have to face the gossip and stares about Billie's disappearing act. But she knew that she would have to face the group eventually, so on Monday morning she put on the new chocolate brown corduroys that her dad had bought her for her birthday, and the yellow turtleneck sweater that Grandma Bootsy had bought her and went on to school.

Well, if no one talks to me at least I can rub my corduroys and sweater and think about Dad and Grandma Bootsy and know that I am loved.

Since starting middle school, she realized that she felt better when she wore something that reminded her of her dad and Grandma Bootsy. On stressful days at school, like test days or days where she had to give presentations, Tanisha always made sure to wear clothing or jewelry that her Dad or Grandma Bootsy had given her to boost her confidence and help calm her nerves.

On Monday, Tanisha was relieved when Lori waved her over to the table as usual. As the girls munched on their cold sandwiches and Tanisha ate her hot lunch sloppy Joe sandwich, their only comments were how much fun the slumber party had been. All of her friends expressed sadness when Tanisha shared that the family's dog Strongest had apparently gotten lost in the blizzard and still hadn't been found.

Tanisha was pleased that her girls were cool with her, but she was still worried that at least a couple of the parents would call Billie at home to express their unhappiness with Billie's poor judgment. In Tanisha's mind, leaving teenage girls unsupervised all night at a sleepover was an unforgivable sin. But a week had passed and as far as she knew, no one had called.

Tanisha checked her reflection again in the mirror and smoothed down her hair. She popped a cinnamon mint in her mouth, threw the pack in her slim line disco purse for later and headed downstairs to wait for Mrs. Perkins.

John & Judy was a Chicago area social organization for dads and their children. Membership in John & Judy was by referral only and most of the dads were doctors, lawyers and business professionals. The fifty year old networking organization was formed to provide a forum for the children of black professionals to socialize, mix and mingle with like minded families. The teen members of John & Judy were required to raise resources for charitable causes and often hosted parties to meet their civic obligation.

All but Grace and Justine were going to the party together. Grace and Justine weren't interested in going to the teen mixer which was just as well because Mrs. Perkins' Caprice Classic only had room for four teenage girls in the back seat. Lori's sister, Charlotte, was a sophomore at River North High School and had received an invitation for the Saturday night teen mixer.

Mrs. Perkins pulled up at 7:15 and Tanisha raced outside as she was pulling her car up to the curb in front of Tanisha's house. She jumped in the backseat with Maria, Lori and Rashanda and said hello to Mrs. Perkins and Charlotte.

"You smell good, Tanisha." Lori inhaled deeply.

"Thanks, Lori. It's the Love's Baby Soft cologne that Grace gave me for my birthday," Tanisha explained.

"It does smell good. I'm gonna have to get some of that for myself," Maria said.

Tanisha was proud that for once she had something that Maria didn't have. The girls giggled and chatted for the fifteen minute ride to Alpine Lake. Charlotte was not attending the party but had convinced all of the girls to give her one dollar towards gas for arranging the carpool. All of the girls knew that the gas contribution was just Charlotte's way of extorting money from Lori's friends and that Mrs. Perkins was unaware of the gas fee, especially when Charlotte pretended to have to use the restroom in order to corner the girls out of view of Mrs. Perkins to collect everyone's dollar. The girls were so happy to be attending a boy-girl party not associated with River North High School that everyone except Lori handed over her dollar without making a fuss.

"Charlotte, I'm telling Ma that you're taking money from my friends," Lori threatened.

"They gave it to me. I didn't take it," Charlotte said folding the bills in her hand.

Charlotte would be taking driver's education in a few weeks, and once she got her license, Lori would have to rely on her older sister for rides. If she told on Charlotte, she could forget getting Charlotte to tote her and her friends to the movies and the mall.

Alpine Lake was a private clubhouse adjacent to a membership only swimming pool and small lake. It was located in the town of Homer and surrounded by modest split level and Georgian styled homes with manicured lawns.

Tanisha and her girls decided to go to the party dressed alike. The girls had all purchased matching rugby shirts in different colors at their last group trip to the mall. Decked out in matching shirts and a spectrum of designer jeans, the party of four paid their three dollars and went in. The girls hung their ski jackets on the hooks lining the entry way.

The music played loudly as the girls slowly entered the dimly lit room. They giggled as they noticed a wall of teenage boys staring at them curiously. Maria whispered, "Let's go to the bathroom to plan our strategy."

"The boys here are too fine!" Maria continued. "Here's the plan. Let's spread out. We'll meet more boys if we are in small groups," she coached. "Rashanda and I will hang out and Tanisha and Lori will hang out." Maria applied a small dab of Vaseline on her lips.

Tanisha giggled at the Vaseline jar, but put a dab on her lips as well. Maria was right. The Vaseline worked better than the lip gloss that she'd been using. *Looks like Dawn knew more than I thought. I wonder how things are working out for her in Texas?*

"Rashanda and I will walk out first, and you and Lori come out after a few minutes," Maria suggested.

Lori and Tanisha waited two minutes before re-joining the party. When they came out of the bathroom, the lights were dimmed and a slow ballad played. Tanisha spanned the room, and she and Lori stood against a wall opposite the disc jockey's table.

There were over eighty teenagers in the party room, a healthy mix of boys and girls. Many of the boys wore Homer Glen High School letterman's jackets. A short boy with a Homer Glen baseball jacket approached and asked Lori to dance. Tanisha shifted her weight from her left foot to her right foot and watched as Lori danced. From across the room she noticed a tall chocolate brown teenager smiling at her. He wore a Homer Glen letterman's jacket with 85 on the sleeve. He smiled at her and waved. Tanisha looked over her shoulder to see if he was waving at someone else. When she turned around, he waved at her again and proceeded to walk over to her.

"Hi. I'm Byron Bird. Would you like to dance?"

Tanisha was caught off guard but mumbled a quiet "Sure."

Byron took her hand and led her to the dance floor as Annie Lennox's song *Sweet Dreams* played. Tanisha thought her knees would buckle.

"You didn't tell me your name. What's your name?" Byron bent down to speak directly into Tanisha's ear. She could feel his warm breath on her neck.

"Oh, I'm sorry. It's Tanisha. My name is Tanisha Carlson." *I can't believe this gorgeous high school guy is interested in me.* "My brother's name is Byron," she offered.

"Your brother must be a pretty cool guy. Where do you go to school, Tanisha?" Byron asked.

"Oh, I'm a freshman at River North," Tanisha said. *I can't tell this cutie that I'm still in middle school!*

"Do you go to Homer Glen?" Tanisha stammered.

"Yeah. I'm a sophomore at HG. But I play on the varsity basketball team."

"How long have you lived in Homer Glen?" Tanisha asked.

"I live in Homer. Homer and Glen are separate cities," Byron said.

Idiot! I knew that! Similarly, River and North were separate cities but the high school shared both names like Homer Glen. *Duh! I know he must think I'm a hillbilly!* She wanted to melt into the floor for her geographic faux pas.

"How do you like River?" Byron asked sweetly. Everyone called River North High School "River" for short.

What? He's still interested enough in me to ask me more questions? She was so relieved that he'd forgiven her Homer Glen one city oversight that she almost peed her pants.

"It's fine." She didn't want too many questions about River since she wasn't a student there yet. But since she was in several ninth grade honors classes, technically she was almost a freshman. Tanisha cast a faint smile at Byron the hottie. *Don't let him see the decayed front fang or he really will think you're a hillbilly.*

With hours of practicing in the mirror, Tanisha had perfected a crooked smile where the right corner of her mouth didn't curl up so that you couldn't see that she had visible tooth decay in her right eye tooth. Since all of her other teeth were white and perfectly aligned, it created the illusion of a perfect smile. The crooked smile made her look demure and coy. Some of her closest friends were unaware of the decayed front tooth, and she wasn't going to flash the cavity at this cutie!

"You have a nice smile." Byron smiled back. His teeth were white and perfectly aligned.

"Thanks. So do you." *If he only knew. This tall chocolate drop is actually flirting with me. Keep him talking.*

"Are you in John & Judy?" Tanisha asked coyly, taking care to hide her tooth as she flirted.

"I'm in the Chicago chapter. We just moved to Homer last year and so my dad is going to stay active with that chapter. Is your dad in John & Judy?"

"No, but my friend Leslie Wood is in the South Suburban chapter. You might know her because she goes to HG," Tanisha said.

"You know Leslie? I know Leslie. She's cool." Byron's body moved in time with the slow beat.

Leslie's dad was a banker and a member of John & Judy. Leslie's parents were divorced and her dad had remarried and lived in Glen with his new family. Although Leslie lived in Cedar Grove with her mother, Leslie took the train to Homer Glen High School every morning since she was able to use her dad's Glen address. Homer Glen was one of the top public high schools in the nation. Leslie and Tanisha had become friends that summer at the Cedar Grove pool. Leslie had helped Tanisha feel better about her parent's separation.

Leslie was best friends with Vicky who lived in Cedar Grove and attended River with Tanisha's older brother Jack. Although Tanisha was friends with Leslie and Vicky in Cedar Grove, they didn't attend Battle Creek Junior High so they weren't friends with Tanisha's Battle Creek Junior High crew. Leslie and Vicky weren't planning to go to the young teen mixer since they were sixteen and Leslie only attended the John & Judy events with the senior teen group.

"Thanks for the dance, Tanisha. Can I call you sometime?" Byron asked.

"Sure. Do you have a pen?" *I can't believe that this boy wants my phone number!*

"I don't, but I'll get one from my older brother. I think he has one in the car. I'll be right back," Byron said.

As Tanisha floated off the dance floor she bumped into Lori who'd been watching from the sidelines.

"He is too fine!" Lori squealed.

"I know. He's a sophomore at HG. I told him I was a freshman at River. So don't bust me out and mention Battle Creek Junior High, okay?"

Byron returned with a pen and a small strip of paper. Tanisha carefully wrote down her phone number. She'd never given her number to a boy before and was excited by the prospect of receiving a phone call at home. Byron tore off a small corner from the paper and wrote down his number and handed it to Tanisha.

"Nice to meet you, Tanisha. I'll call you sometime," Byron offered.

"Okay. It was nice to meet you too, Byron," Tanisha replied.

Tanisha could have floated out of the room. As far as she was concerned, the party was over and she needed to get home to catch that phone call. Tanisha was so smitten that she didn't plan to dance with any other boys the rest of the evening. She didn't want to run the risk of making Byron jealous.

The party ended a few minutes later and Rashanda's mom picked the girls up in their new light green Lincoln Town Car.

Tanisha breathed a sigh of relief. *Thank goodness Mrs. Jordan drove the Lincoln, because their second car is a beat up Ford Torino and I did not want Byron to see me climbing into the back of a beat up car.*

As the girls piled into the backseat of the car, Rashanda pleaded with her mom to take them to White Castle for the "after party," but her mom wasn't having any of that. At the end of the party, when the lights came on, the sixteen and over crowd was coordinating their trip to White Castle for the after party where the boys would eat burgers and get phone numbers. Tanisha suspected that Byron might be at White Castle and longed to see him again, but Rashanda's mom reminded the group that it was almost eleven o'clock at night so she dropped them off at their homes.

As Rashanda's mom guided her car up to Tanisha's Cedar Grove townhouse, Tanisha snapped out of her Byron daydream. The large vehicle pulled to a graceful stop in front of the plain townhouses lined four in a row with the cars parked in the front.

Tanisha thought that the complex resembled a low income housing unit. And why shouldn't it? That's exactly what it was.

Tanisha waved at her friends and walked quickly up the stairs, her mood soured. *Will Byron still be interested in me when he finds out where I live?*

Chapter 4

Boys Will Be Boys

Byron hadn't called. It had been two weeks since the John & Judy party at Alpine Lake, and Tanisha hadn't heard from him. Of course her BCJH girls assured her that he'd probably just lost her number, and that since Billie insisted on having an unlisted phone number, he had no way of reaching her.

But in her heart, Tanisha knew that wasn't true. Leslie went to Homer Glen High School and Byron could have asked her for Tanisha's number if he'd lost it. No, he wasn't really interested in her. *He probably thinks I'm not good enough for him. Or he only dates girls whose dads are in John & Judy, and since my dad is just an electrician I'm not his type. But how would he know any of this? He probably asked Leslie and she told him. But Leslie is my friend.*

Tanisha was smitten. She daydreamed about Byron and spent idle time doodling his name in her notebook. He had also given her his telephone number and she considered calling him first.

Tanisha ran her dilemma by her peers at lunch.

"He still hasn't called me. Why did he ask for my number if he wasn't going to call me?" Tanisha whined.

"You should just call him. He did give you his number," Lori said.

"You shouldn't call him first. The boy should call the girl first or he'll think that you're fast," Maria explained.

"But what if he lost my number? We're not listed, and he could have lost that little slip of paper," Tanisha suggested.

"He could get your number from Leslie." Maria took a sip from her milk carton.

He probably threw my number away after he found out that my dad is an electrician. Tanisha took a bite from her apple. Maria was right. Tanisha didn't want him to think that she was fast. But she really wanted to talk to him. She'd never had a boyfriend before and couldn't stop thinking about Byron and longing for him to call her. She held onto his number and even memorized it 555-9137. But she was too nervous to call him.

Tanisha was struggling with popularity in middle school even though she was on the pom pon squad and ran track at Battle Creek Junior High. She was also a student council representative and a straight A student in honors classes. Nonetheless, Tanisha hadn't attracted attention from any of the boys at her school. Battle Creek Junior High School was predominantly white but the few black boys that attended were either interested in Maria with her long wavy hair and designer clothes or the white girls at school.

As she ate her lunch, Tanisha's thoughts drifted to Keith Kyals.

The year before when she was twelve, just three months shy of her thirteenth birthday, Tanisha attended a birthday party for Keith Kyals with her older brother Jack. Keith Kyals was the star of the sophomore baseball team and the sophomore class president. He had seen Tanisha at a River North High School play with Jack and had asked Jack to invite his sister, so Jack obliged. He didn't want to bring his kid sister to a high school party, but Keith was one of the most popular boys at River. Tanisha was the only middle school student at the birthday party. Tanisha hadn't attended a boy girl party before, and without her friends, she didn't know what she was supposed to do. The other girls at the party glared at Tanisha and whispered about her. She could still hear their questions.

"Who is she?"

"*Does she go to River?*"

"*Isn't she a seventh grader at Battle Creek?*"

"*Yup! That's Jack Carlson's little sister. I heard Keith say that he asked Jack to invite her.*"

"*Oh! Keith likes her. She's cute, but she's only in seventh grade.*"

And so the comments continued throughout the night. Jack entertained himself with his friends. Tanisha sat quietly in a corner of the dimly lit family room, sipping on punch and munching pizza wondering why she had been invited to the party. None of the other boys had asked her to dance since the rumor had circulated that Tanisha's presence had been requested by Keith. The other boys were afraid to speak to Tanisha at the risk of disrespecting Keith at his own party. Just as Tanisha was about to feign a headache and ask Jack to call their Mom to pick them up, Keith walked over and started talking to her.

"*You're Jack's sister, Tanisha, right? Thanks for coming to my party. Are you having a good time?*" *Keith smiled.*

"*Yes. Thanks for inviting me. Happy Birthday,*" *Tanisha giggled.*

"*Sorry I haven't danced with you all night. Since I'm the host, my mom has me running around a lot,*" *Keith explained.*

"*Oh. That's okay. I could see that you were busy,*" *Tanisha said. She'd seen him mingling with his relatives in the kitchen when she and Jack arrived. He'd smiled and waved at Jack as his mom escorted them to the small family room.*

"*I saw you at Fiddler on the Roof. I play saxophone in the jazz band. One of my boys in the band told me that you were Jack Carlson's little sister,*" *Keith said.*

"*Oh. Is band fun?*" *Tanisha asked nervously.*

"*It's cool, but I'm ready to quit the instrument now, but my pops won't let me. Let's dance.*"

Keith grabbed Tanisha's hand and pulled her into the center of the family room. Barry White's Ecstasy played. It was the first time that a boy had ever asked Tanisha to slow dance and Tanisha wasn't sure what to do with her hands, so she watched the other couples and placed her hands over Keith's shoulders the way the other girls did. Keith smelled of Ralph Lauren Polo cologne and 7-Up. His body was warm against hers and his breath smelled like spearmint gum. As Tanisha enjoyed his scent, Keith placed his hands around her waist and pulled her closer into his body and playfully whispered. "Relax, I won't bite you."

Tanisha smiled sweetly and immediately felt something firm pressing against her body just below her waist. She was shocked at first but she did not pull away.

She wondered if others in the room could see that Keith was pressed firmly against her body and that his hands had slipped from the lower part of her back down to her buttocks. She was grateful that the room was dark so that others couldn't see where Keith's hands were resting. Tanisha didn't know what to do. She'd never slow danced with a boy before and didn't know what to expect. Her thoughts raced as Keith's lower body moved in perfect rhythm to Barry White's deep baritone voice.

Their bodies were welded together as one as Keith continued to rotate his hips in a counter clockwise motion into Tanisha's body. Not sensing any resistance to their closeness, Keith embraced Tanisha even tighter and gently rotated his hips into her pelvis in a steady rhythm as his spearmint breath danced across her neck. Tanisha had never experienced this feeling before and didn't have words to describe it, but she knew that dancing with Keith felt good to her and that she didn't want the song to end.

But it did end. Keith thanked her for the dance. "I'll see you later, gorgeous," he whispered.

Tanisha floated back to her corner spot in the recreation room while Keith continued to dance with the other girls at the party. When the party ended, he said a polite goodbye. Although she wasn't physically attracted to Keith, (at five feet seven inches he wasn't tall enough for her taste) she had enjoyed slow dancing with him and was surprised that he hadn't asked for her phone number. She knew from her older friends that after you slow danced with a boy, if he liked you, he asked for your phone number. She would think about that dance every time she heard Barry White's Ecstasy. Tanisha tried to duplicate the slow dance experience using rolled up towels and her blanket imagining herself slow dancing with Byron Bird.

"Earth calling Tanisha! You're always daydreaming, girl. Snap out of it! Did you hear me?" Lori snapped her fingers in Tanisha's face.

"I'm sorry. What did you say?" Tanisha asked.

"I said that you shouldn't worry about that Byron dude anymore because Darrell Hunter likes you," Lori repeated.

"How do you know?" Tanisha brightened.

Darrell Hunter was one of the most popular boys at Battle Creek Junior High. He was captain of the eighth grade basketball team, president of the student council and he excelled at track, helping the team win their conference division in seventh grade.

Tanisha was also on the track team and had placed third in the high jump competition and ran anchor on the winning four hundred meter relay team. At the seventh grade regional conference, Darrell had complimented Tanisha on a well run race.

"I heard Darrell tell CJ that he thought that you were cute," Lori explained.

CJ Odom and Darrell were best friends. CJ and Lori had been going together for three weeks.

"Are you sure he was talking about me?" Tanisha couldn't believe her good fortune. *Why would Darrell Hunter like me?*

"You're the only Tanisha Carlson at Battle Creek aren't you? You should ask him to the Turnabout dance!"

Tanisha hadn't planned to go to the Turnabout dance, but if Darrell Hunter liked her, then she just might have to ask him.

Turnabout was Battle Creek's annual Sadie Hawkins dance where the girls asked the boys, bought the tickets and paid for the meal after the dance. Tanisha hadn't gone to Turnabout in seventh grade, but Lori and Maria had gone and had given a full report the following Monday at school on who had been kissing whom. According to Lori and Maria's account, the Turnabout Dance was a lip locking festival.

"Wait a minute. I thought Darrell liked Tracy Jones?" Tanisha asked.

An average student, Tracy Jones' popularity overshadowed her academic limitations. Since transferring to Battle Creek from St. Louis, Missouri during the second semester of seventh grade, Tracy's womanly curves and bra size had been a hit with the teenage boys at school. Their heads turned as she sashayed through the hallway, her hips moving as though performing a figure eight with her backside. Her dad's status as a promising executive with IBM provided the family a solid financial cushion, one that comfortably supported Tracy's designer jeans fetish and her mother's wanderlust for travel, an appetite she developed as a model. This sweetened Tracy's allure as the most interesting girl to grace the halls of Battle Creek Junior High. Tracy often boasted about her mother's frequent jaunts to Paris, London and Ethiopia. Although she was no longer a model, Mrs. Jones scouted promising talent for a New York agency. Certainly not the brightest bulb in the chandelier, Tracy was cute, popular, upper middle class, well dressed, and her parents led glamorous lifestyles.

Tanisha envied Tracy. Everything about her life was enviable, except her grades. The boys wanted to date her, and the girls wanted to dress like her, wear their hair like her, and be her friend. Including Tanisha.

But Tracy Jones didn't like Tanisha. Her attempts to be friendly with Tracy were rudely ignored or rebuffed. Thinking it her imagination, Tanisha involved her friends who asked around and confirmed this truth. Tracy didn't like Tanisha. No explanation was provided. Her response had been simple and curt, "I don't like Tanisha." Tracy had recently hosted a boy-girl birthday party at her home and had invited all of the "popular" eighth grade students including Tanisha's circle of friends.

Tanisha didn't understand why Tracy had apparently singled her out and snubbed her at her party. Tracy was in Lori's math and science class and shared the same home room adviser (Mrs. Taylor) with Lori, Maria, Rashanda, and Grace.

Mrs. Taylor was one of only two African American teachers at Battle Creek Junior High and the principal always honored requests for any African American girls who wanted to switch home room advisers to join Mrs. Taylor or Mrs. James' home room sections. Tanisha had Mrs. Shay, the elderly white librarian as her home room adviser. Mrs. Shay was very nice and Tanisha really liked her and didn't want to hurt her feelings or offend her by switching advisers, even to join the mini sorority that was Mrs. Taylor's group.

"Tracy just doesn't know you, Tanisha," Rashanda had suggested. "Since you're not in Mrs. Taylor's home room, and she's not in any of your classes, Tracy just hasn't gotten a chance to get to know you," she continued.

"That's right," Lori had agreed. "I'm sure that's what it is."

Justine had been reading and lifted her head above her book casually. "That can't be the reason," she said. "I'm not in Mrs. Taylor's home room, and I don't have any classes with Tracy either, but she invited me," Justine said casually. "There must be another reason," she finished. "Ouch! Why did you kick me, Maria?"

Tanisha smiled at her friends' kind attempts to explain why she was being snubbed. "It's okay, you guys. Don't feel bad for me," she offered stoically. "Tracy just doesn't like me. I didn't do anything to her, and I'm not going to chase behind her like a puppy to find out why she doesn't like me," she shrugged. "I'll get over it. Go ahead and go to the party and tell me what it's like," she finished, forcing herself to smile when she really wanted to weep. Much to Tanisha's despair, the party had been a huge hit, complete with a professional disc jockey and waiters. It was dubbed the party of the year, pouring salt in Tanisha's wound that she'd not been invited.

Tanisha continued to be friendly when she saw Tracy, but Tracy usually just ignored her. Over time, the obvious eye rolling and deliberate glares discouraged Tanisha from feigning even the simplest civility toward her. Her obvious rudeness angered Tanisha. *I didn't do anything to this girl for her to treat me like this! That's why she's a C student in basic math and science classes!*

"I think Tracy likes him," Lori said. "But I don't think that he likes her. I'd know if he did. CJ would have mentioned it to me. You should ask him to Turnabout," Lori encouraged.

Is this why Tracy Jones hates my guts? She likes Darrell Hunter, but he likes me? "I don't know if I'm ready to ask him. What if he says no, Lori?" Tanisha wasn't in the mood for rejection on a Monday morning.

"Tell you what. I'll ask CJ to find out if Darrell is going with anybody to the dance. If he isn't, I'll ask him to find out if he would say yes if you asked him. Cool?" Lori was excited that CJ had asked her to "go with him" and was looking forward to the Turnabout Dance.

Although most of Tanisha's crew was turning fourteen that year, none of them had ever kissed a boy before except Maria. Maria was very popular with the boys and had kissed a boy in sixth grade.

So it was agreed that Lori would have CJ scout out Darrell's response to pave the way for Tanisha to ask him to the dance. Tanisha knew that she would have to call Lori that evening since she wouldn't see her again for the rest of the day. There were two more class periods before the dismissal buzzer sounded, and Tanisha had typing and algebra remaining on her schedule.

The rest of the day dragged on. Tanisha whizzed through her typing class and again won the mini competition on who could type the paragraph the fastest. Tanisha was an excellent typist and could type almost eighty words per minute with less than five errors. Billie was an administrative assistant and could type over one hundred words per minute with less than five errors so Tanisha knew that she had inherited Billie's quick typing speed.

The only person in the class that gave her a run for her money on the IBM electric typewriter was Larry Colbert. Larry was the class whiz kid and excelled at all things academic. He was in all of Tanisha's honors classes and had been in her homeroom class since third grade at Mahala Elementary School. Since their last names were close, Larry and Tanisha's lockers were always near each other and Tanisha knew that Larry seldom took home books to study. He would take home any homework assignments but he never studied. Larry was a genius. Tanisha was pleased that she was a better typist than Larry. She was proud of her academic success and glad that she was finally slightly better at something than Larry whom she considered a friend.

Larry had typed the paragraph as quickly as Tanisha but had made six errors to Tanisha's five errors. Tanisha knew that Larry was anxious to beat her at typing and that she would have to trim her nails to ensure that her fingers slid smoothly along the keyboard for the final exam.

Larry and Tanisha walked the fifteen steps from the typing lab to their algebra class. Battle Creek Junior High was a modern school concept where there were no walls separating the classrooms. The only dividers were chalk boards or file cabinets that rolled along on coasters so that the classrooms could be modified easily. The Math department consisted of one large area that was separated into four different open classrooms. The Social Studies, Science and English departments were set-up in the same fashion. Even the media center or library was without walls. The only areas that had traditional walls and doors were the foreign language department, Typing room, Art, Industrial Arts, Home Economics, Music and Physical Education. When Tanisha first arrived at Battle Creek, the chatter from the neighboring classrooms proved a distraction to her, especially during test days. But now, just one year later, Tanisha enjoyed the openness of the school.

The math and science teachers had a pod of offices surrounded by windows so the math teachers could see the math department and the science teachers could see the science department from their desks. Darrell Hunter had science for seventh period and often went into the office to make copies for Mrs. Taylor. Occasionally, Tanisha could catch a glimpse of Darrell making copies, so she often glanced in that direction hoping that she would see him. Today, Mrs. James caught her staring at the office window a little too intently and snapped her out of her daydream.

"Ms. Carlson! The blackboard is over here! Tell you what, since you seem to be daydreaming, why don't you go to the board and do the next problem?" Mrs. James barked.

Although her statement was phrased like a question, Tanisha knew that it was a direct order. Mrs. James often referred to students by their last name. No one knew why, it was just her thing. Mrs. James had a glass eye in the left socket, so when she looked at you, you didn't know for sure if she was looking at you. No one knew exactly what happened that caused her to lose an eye, not even some of the teachers. Tanisha's older brother Jack and one of his classmates had nicknamed Mrs. James "Disco Eye" since her glass eye resembled a strobe light because it often rolled around in the socket.

Aaargh! It never fails! Mrs. James always calls me to the board when I have on a busted outfit. She never calls me to the board when I have on my Calvin Klein jeans.

Mrs. James was always immaculately dressed. She was a petite woman and was able to wear her teenage daughter's clothes, so Mrs. James' wardrobe was extensive. She only repeated an outfit every three or four months if that. She walked quickly to the black board and picked up a piece of chalk. Tanisha was doing well in algebra so she completed the problem correctly and quickly took her seat.

It's a good thing Darrell isn't in my algebra class. I'll wear my Calvins tomorrow in case I run into him again at lunchtime.

The bus ride home seemed to last forever. Due to construction on Western Avenue, the bus driver was forced to drive Hawkeye Drive. Tanisha always enjoyed driving through Newberry East because she was able to admire the modest split level and small Georgian homes that lined Hickok Lodge. Darrell Hunter's family lived near Hickok Lodge and if Tanisha strained her neck, she could see Darrell's house from the bus. She longed to move from the Cedar Grove complex and wondered how that would be possible now that her parents were getting divorced.

As soon as Tanisha got off the school bus in Cedar Grove that afternoon she raced to the phone to call Lori. Her brothers were watching *Tom and Jerry* in the living room and Tanisha mumbled a quick hello to them on her way to the kitchen. She picked up the receiver in the kitchen and couldn't get a dial tone. She clicked it a few times.

The kitchen cord is always shorting out! Allen and Byron are just going to have to hear this conversation. I can't wait until I've saved enough money to buy that pink Princess phone for my room.

Tanisha raced into the living room and picked up the Snoopy character phone that also served as a table lamp. No dial tone on that phone either. The handset against her ear, she took a long, deliberate breath and exhaled slowly. Tanisha knew what it meant, but she couldn't believe it. She didn't want to believe it. *Please, God! Not again! Not again!*

Chapter 5

Call Me Sometime

The phone was disconnected. This was the third time within the school year that the telephone had been turned off.

I wonder how much the bill is this time! Billie wasn't in the habit of paying bills in a timely fashion. Since her parent's separation, two eviction notices had been delivered to their home, and the electric bill usually had a red late notice inside of it. Billie made an average wage at her job as a secretary at the local community college and received money every week from the children's father, Jackie, but she managed money like a child. *They should just pay her in beer and cigarettes since that's what she spends her money on!*

Tanisha was dying to know if CJ had asked Darrell about the Turnabout Dance! She ran to her room and tossed out the coins from her clear glass piggy bank. She had exactly eighty-three cents in change. She scooped up the coins and raced down the stairs and out the kitchen door headed to the pay phone by the Cedar Grove pool and clubhouse. If she called Lori from the pay phone before Lori tried to call her, perhaps she could save herself the embarrassment of telling her friend that their phone was disconnected.

She grabbed the payphone and counted to ten to catch her breath. She dropped two dimes into the slot and dialed Lori's number from memory.

"Hi, Mrs. Perkins. This is Tanisha. How are you?"

"I'm fine, Tanisha. How are you?" Mrs. Perkins asked.

"I'm fine. May I speak to Lori, please?" Tanisha asked.

"Sure. Hold on for a minute."

Tanisha was panicked that she would run out of change before Lori got to the phone. It had been twenty-cents to initiate the call and the recorded message had told her that it would be twenty-cents for each additional five minutes.

"Hey, Tanisha," Lori sounded chipper.

"Hey, Lori. Did you try to call me?" Tanisha asked curiously.

"I did. But I got a message that your phone was temporarily disconnected."

"Yeah, something's wrong with our phone. I can make calls out but we can't receive any calls. It's weird," Tanisha lied.

"Well, what did CJ find out?" Tanisha knew that she had enough change to talk for fifteen minutes.

"CJ told me that Darrell said that he would say yes if you asked him!"

Tanisha couldn't believe it. Darrell Hunter wanted to go to the dance with her. "Really? When should I ask him?" she squealed.

"You should ask him tomorrow, girl!" Lori didn't let grass grow under her feet.

"Okay! Good idea! Lori, I need to let you go so my mother can call the phone company and see what's wrong with our phone. I'll look for you tomorrow before first period so you can help me script what I should say," Tanisha finished.

"Okay. I'll see you tomorrow."

Tanisha grinned all the way home. She hadn't had to put any more money in the phone and Lori had believed her story that their phone only made outside calls.

She stopped dead in her tracks as it hit her. When she asked Darrell to the Turnabout dance, he would ask for her telephone number. She couldn't ask Darrell to the dance until her phone was turned back on. Tanisha had to get the phone turned back on as soon as possible.

Her shoulders hunched, she walked slowly to her room to plan her strategy. As she made it to the top of the stairs she saw Billie crawling into her bed with a freshly lit Virginia Slims menthol cigarette and the latest Cosmopolitan magazine.

"Hi, Mom, you're home early. Did you just get in?"

Billie took a pull from her cigarette and muttered. "Hello. Yes, I did."

Tanisha was trying desperately to sound chipper. "How was work today?"

Billie continued to ruffle the magazines scattered across her bed and responded without looking at Tanisha. "I wasn't feeling well so I didn't go to work."

Tanisha suspected that Billie had been fired from her job at Eden State College or she was deliberately trying to get fired due to the number of sick days that she'd taken recently.

Tanisha tried to speak to Billie as infrequently as possible but she knew that she had to engage her mother in conversation to find out about the telephone.

"I hope you're feeling better. Mom, did you know that the phone isn't working?" Tanisha asked as sweetly as she could.

Billie glanced up from the top of her magazine and took a puff from her Virginia Slims menthol. "I know. It's disconnected," she stated flatly.

"Will it be turned back on tomorrow?" Tanisha asked desperately.

"I'm not getting it turned back on right away." Billie replied cavalierly without glancing up from her magazine.

"Why not?" Tanisha pleaded. "What if there's an emergency?"

"I don't have the money for the phone, Tanisha! If there's an emergency, we can just use Mr. Preston's phone next door." Billie glared at Tanisha and took a long drag from her cigarette.

Use Mr. Preston's phone next door? That would never work. How could she give Darrell Mr. Preston's phone number to call her? Didn't Billie know that the telephone was Tanisha's lifeline to civilization? Didn't her mother care that her social standing was already in quick sand and that it would sink without a telephone?

"How much is the phone bill?" Tanisha whispered fighting back tears in her voice.

"It's eighty two dollars." Billie was now flipping through her Cosmopolitan magazine and only paused long enough to take another puff from her cigarette.

"Won't they turn it back on if we pay half of it?" Tanisha had been down this road with Billie a few times before and knew that the phone company would turn the service back on if at least half of the bill were paid in cash.

"I don't have **half** of it, Tanisha!" Billie was not in a negotiating mood.

"Well, didn't Dad just give you the child support money?" Tanisha knew that this was a hot button with Billie. Tanisha's father paid child support, but it was usually gone so quickly that Tanisha and her brothers couldn't account for how Billie spent the money.

Billie now looked up from her magazine and glared at Tanisha. "Not that it's any of your **DAMN** business little girl, but I had to pay the rent, Tanisha!" Billie said angrily.

"Well, I have money left over from my birthday gifts and babysitting, so I can pay half of it to get it turned back on." Tanisha had received belated birthday cards with checks inside from her dad's three sisters almost two months after her birthday. Their gifts were usually very belated, but the cash was always appreciated. Tanisha had planned to use the money to buy a pair of jeans. As much as Tanisha hated to part with her own money, her social status depended on her having a phone. The ruse that she could make external calls but not receive calls wouldn't last longer than one more day. She wouldn't ask Darrell Hunter to the dance until she had a working telephone number.

"Fine! I don't care one way or the other." Billie grunted and snubbed out her cigarette butt in the gold ashtray. The ashtray teetered on the edge of a cardboard box that doubled as Billie's nightstand.

"Can you drop me off at the phone company so I can pay it now? This way they can turn it back on tomorrow," Tanisha pleaded.

Billie let out a loud sigh. "I'm going to my Buddhist meeting, and my meeting is in the other direction. I can't take you or I'll be late."

Tanisha couldn't believe it. She knew that she could take the last Cedar Grove shuttle bus to the grocery store. The shuttle bus was the free bus service for the Cedar Grove adult residents, but the bus driver always let Tanisha and her brothers ride if it wasn't crowded. The phone company was one block from the grocery store. Tanisha would have to pay to take the transit bus home. She glanced at her watch. It was already ten after four. The phone company closed at five o'clock. She turned around to run to her room and grab her money.

"I'll drop you off, but you'll have to take the bus back, Tanisha," Billie grumbled.

Tanisha rushed to her room to get money from her private stash of cash. She reached in the pocket of her cardigan sweater and pulled out her dad's old black sock. She'd found the sock under the sofa one day while vacuuming and had cried softly to herself. She'd washed the sock and tucked it into her sweater pocket for safe keeping. She missed her dad. She squeezed the sock tightly. She'd never managed to save more than sixty dollars before tapping into her stash for one thing or another, and now she was about to surrender over two thirds of her money. She hesitated for a moment. The phone was an emergency. The new jeans could wait. She exhaled loudly, stuffing the few remaining bills into the sock, and back into the tattered sweater. Tucking the forty four dollars into her pocket, she raced downstairs, remembering to grab the phone bill so that she could take it to the clerk.

Tanisha and Billie did not say a word to one another on the six minute ride to the phone company. Once there, Tanisha mumbled thanks and jumped out of the car and raced inside as Billie peeled away in her new car. A few days before, Billie had purchased the used luxury vehicle so that Jack could drive "the Blue Goose" to and from his swing choir rehearsals and job as a bank teller. Tanisha raced inside and ran up to a friendly looking phone clerk.

Good, this clerk is new and won't recognize me from a few months ago.

The clerk's nametag read Rose. When Tanisha approached the counter, Rose smiled at her. "May I help you?" Rose asked.

"My sister's name is Rose. It's one of my favorite names," Tanisha lied. She smiled at the phone clerk as she reached into her small purse. "Anyway, my mother gave me the phone bill and said that she spoke with someone who said that it would be okay to pay half of the bill now." Tanisha twirled the straps of her disco pouch waiting for Rose's response.

Rose took the phone bill and punched several numbers into her computer. Moments later, Rose looked up and informed Tanisha that she would have to pay the entire amount since the phone was turned off and the account had a history of late payments. Tanisha was devastated. Tears swelled in her eyes as she softly asked Rose if there was anything else that she could do.

Rose smiled warmly at Tanisha and told her that she had two options. First, she could plead a hardship to the customer service center by placing a call to them on the house phone. Rose told her that if there was a medical hardship in the household, the phone company would turn the telephone back on if at least half of the balance was paid. The second option was that she could register for a new phone number that would be turned on within twenty four hours. She also winked at Tanisha and told her that she would have to put the new phone number in a different name since the current phone number had a poor payment history. Tanisha asked her how much a new phone number would be per month. Rose informed her that if she had a basic call plan where she didn't call outside of the area code it would be thirteen dollars per month, but if she called outside of the calling area, there would be additional costs.

Tanisha thought about her options. She could get a phone installed in her name and monitor the usage and pay for it every month out of the money she earned at her new part-time job at Save Mart. Two weeks earlier, she'd lied on the application and written that she was fifteen so that she could get a part-time job. She also made anywhere between seven and ten dollars per week babysitting on weekends. Once she paid for her lunch and roller skating, she always had at least two or three dollars left. If she saved this money every month, she could pay the phone bill. Or she could lie and plead a medical hardship to the phone company and beg them to turn on the existing line with the forty dollars toward the outstanding balance. Deep down Tanisha knew that there was really only one solution. She would have to get a new phone number in her name. Anything short of that, and she would continue to be haunted by the quarterly disconnection demon and her social life would suffer.

Tanisha smiled at Rose and told her that she would like to have a line turned on in her name. Rose smiled sweetly and informed her that she would have to be at least sixteen in order to have a phone turned on in her name. "Are you sixteen?" she asked.

"Yes. I just turned sixteen," Tanisha lied.

"May I see your license?" Rose asked.

"I haven't gotten my driver's license yet because I'm still taking Driver's Education. I'm a junior at River North High School." Tanisha didn't know how far this lie was going to go, but she had to play along.

"Oh! My son goes to River North! His name is John Dunn, he's a sophomore. Do you know him?"

"No. I don't know too many sophomores," Tanisha continued.

"I know how that is. I remember when I was in high school I didn't pay attention to the underclassmen." Rose was now typing in the information to get the phone turned on. "I see on the file that this address has already been wired for two lines. This way they won't have to do any wiring inside the house. Were you aware of that?"

Tanisha's room had a phone jack that was not connected to the family's main line. Tanisha tried to plug a phone into the jack in her room but could not get a dial tone from the family's primary number.

"This works out great! My dad was planning to get me my own line as a sweet sixteen present anyway, so I'll just tell him that I took care of it, and he can pay me back," she paused. "My parents are divorced now, and my mom doesn't want me to have my own line, but my dad is going to pay for it. It's a pretty messy divorce," Tanisha fibbed.

"I know. Divorce is so messy for the kids. That's a nice sweet sixteen present. My daughter talks on the phone constantly!" Rose typed into the computer. "Okay, Tanisha. Your new line will be turned on by eight o'clock tomorrow morning, and your new number is 555-5589. Is there anything else that I can do for you?"

"No. Thank you, Rose. You've been very helpful," Tanisha said anxiously.

Tanisha raced to the grocery store in time to catch the bus. Settling into her seat, she was happy that a telephone would be installed the next morning, but her joy was quickly clouded by dread as she thought about Billie's reaction. *Will she be angry that I got a phone turned on in my name? I'll just explain that it was the only solution.*

Tanisha gazed out the window and rehearsed her story to Billie. As she moved her lips quietly, a charcoal gray Chrysler New Yorker pulled alongside of the bus. Tanisha's eyes nearly popped out of the socket as she strained to try and read the license plate. *Maybe Mom felt sorry for me and swung by to pick me up after all!* She pressed her nose against the glass and waved frantically, trying to get her mother's attention. She scowled. The driver was a male. Tanisha slumped back into her seat as the bus swerved away from the curb.

Chapter 6

Dress Rehearsal

The next day, Tanisha made sure to slide a quarter in her pocket so that she could check to see that the phone was turned on. She hadn't seen Lori before the first period bell rang, so she would have to wait until lunch to plan her Turnabout dance strategy. During second period, she asked for a restroom pass and sneaked to the payphones in the cafeteria hallway to call her new number. On her way to the payphone she had a bright idea. *If I stop in the office and tell the secretary that I need to call my mom, she'll let me use the office phone for free, and I won't have to spend my quarter!*

Tanisha was in luck! The office secretary wasn't behind the desk, but the student office aide was. Tanisha recognized the office aide as Beth Taylor, a girl from her home room class. When Beth saw Tanisha she smiled widely showing a mouth full of silver braces with small yellow and red rubber bands connecting from her top teeth to her lower teeth.

Tanisha spoke first. "Hi, Beth!"

"Hi, Tanisha. Nice shirt. What brings you to the office?" Beth asked.

Beth was a nice girl, but she wasn't in any of Tanisha's honors classes, and Tanisha hadn't really gotten to know her. She wasn't athletic and she was exceedingly plain with long stringy brown hair, a mouth full of braces and she wore Sears Roebuck & Company tuff skin jeans. Beth's family lived on a farm in North, and she often came to school smelling of the cattle that she helped tend. Nonetheless, Tanisha always spoke to Beth, and Beth was always nice to Tanisha whenever she saw her.

"Thanks, Beth. I need to call my mom and confirm my orthodontist appointment. Looks like I may be getting braces too," Tanisha lied. She crossed her fingers behind her back. She was getting pretty good at the little white lie game.

"You poor thing, Tanisha! I hate these braces, but they should be coming off in two years. I hope you're not going to Dr. Pavlicka. He's a pain doctor! He kills you when it's time to tighten the wires. And pray you don't have to wear those tiny squirrel or rabbit rubber bands. Those are the worst," Beth groaned.

"I think I'm going to Dr. Pavlicka, but I'm not sure." Tanisha walked behind the desk, dialed the number that she had already memorized, and prayed that it rang. She held her breath in anticipation. It rang! Tanisha exhaled and took a deep breath.

She let the phone ring four times before she hung up. "There's no answer. My mom must have gone to the store," she squealed. "Thanks for letting me use the phone, Beth! I like your jeans by the way! See you in homeroom!" She stopped briefly in the restroom and applied more strawberry lip gloss to her lips just in case she ran into Darrell.

So far so good. I can't wait for lunch so that Lori and I can coordinate what I'm going to say to Darrell!

Tanisha always ate lunch with Lori, Rashanda and Maria during the first mod. Justine and Grace ate lunch during the third lunch mod. The lunch hour was broken into three twenty minute modules or "mods" in order to accommodate all of the middle school students. Tanisha was always so hungry by lunchtime that she was grateful that her schedule allowed her to eat during the first twenty minute "mod."

The lunch menu was a hot ham and cheese sandwich, French fries and cling peaches. Tanisha grabbed a small chocolate milk container, paid for her lunch and sat next to Rashanda.

Rashanda always had the same lunch: a ham and cheese sandwich on whole wheat bread cut into two long rectangles, a small sandwich bag filled with potato chips, a green apple or sometimes a golden delicious apple, a few chocolate chip cookies and a piece of peppermint or butterscotch candy.

If Rashanda wasn't that hungry and couldn't finish her lunch, she would offer half of her sandwich to Tanisha. Rashanda's mom made the best ham and cheese sandwiches and put just the right amount of mayonnaise on the bread.

Tanisha hoped that Rashanda wasn't that hungry today. She hated the hot ham and cheese sandwich. The bread was soggy and the cheese was burned. She pushed the sandwich aside and ate her fries.

Lori couldn't wait to ask Tanisha if she'd seen Darrell. "So! Have you seen him today?"

Tanisha was in a jovial mood. "Have I seen whom?" she quipped sarcastically. An English whiz, she tried to always use pronouns correctly.

"Har! Har! Very funny! You know WHO I'm talking about! Give up the dirt, girl!" Lori said.

Rashanda took a sip from her chocolate milk. "Well, I don't know who you're talking about. What's up?"

"Tanisha didn't tell you? CJ told me that Darrell wants Tanisha to ask him to the Turnabout dance!" Lori squealed.

"Oh, that's cool!" Rashanda said.

"I just found out yesterday, but I didn't get a chance to call you because my mother was dealing with the phone company for a long time and then it was too late to call. Our phone box is at the bottom of the hill behind our house, and it got hit by a car, so yesterday we couldn't receive calls but we could make calls. It was weird. Anyway, crazy Billie ranted and raved with them for a long time and demanded that we have phone service within twenty-four hours. And they told her that the only way we could have phone service within twenty-four hours was to get a new phone number assigned, so let me give you guys my new phone number now before I forget," Tanisha lied again.

Tanisha pulled out a piece of notebook paper and cut it into six strips and wrote her name and new phone number on each strip.

"I won't see Grace and Justine for the rest of the day, so will you give these to them on the bus, Lori?"

"Sure! So when are you planning to ask Darrell? You look cute today so you should definitely ask him today," Lori encouraged. She was convinced that Tanisha had to strike while the iron was hot!

"Thanks! I was going to ask him at pom pon rehearsal tomorrow. I usually see him before the boys start basketball practice. I planned to wear my Calvins and my new hoodie. What do you think?" Tanisha knew that was when she would do it but wanted the approval of her girls.

"That's a good idea! And after he says yes we can do a cheer!" Maria giggled.

Maria was the first black cheerleader to make the eighth grade cheerleading squad. She hated being the only girl of color on the squad, but her parents had encouraged her to try out.

Tanisha was at Maria's house the day her parents encouraged her to tryout and remembered their comments.

"You're a gymnast, and you can do all of the flips and jumps that are required. It's shameful that no black girls have ever been selected for the cheerleading squad," they stated. "Maria, you will be known as a trail blazer if you make it. Besides, once more blacks move to the area,

other girls will try out and make it. And you'll be remembered forever as the first," Mr. Wesley encouraged. "And if you don't make it, your mom and I will be meeting with the principal," he shared.

Maria had made the squad without her parent's intervention, but she hated it. She wanted to be on the pom pon squad with Tanisha and Lori.

"But you should try to see him before we change into our P.E. uniforms so that he can see how cute you look," Lori encouraged.

"Good point!" Tanisha hadn't considered that aspect of the timing. The P.E. uniform was a navy blue twill one piece jump suit. Tanisha was five feet seven inches tall and wore a size five jeans so she looked good in her P.E. uniform, but it wasn't as cute as her snug fitting Calvins. "If I race to the gym right after algebra, I should see him for a minute before he goes into the locker room to change for basketball practice."

Tanisha knew that it would be cutting it close. She seldom saw Darrell before pom pon practice but usually saw him while the boys' basketball team was practicing and the girls were working on their pom pon routine in the upper loft portion of the gymnasium.

"Does anyone want the rest of my sandwich?" Rashanda offered.

"I'll take it if no one else wants it," Tanisha offered.

"Go for it. I'm trying to watch my weight because Todd says that I'm getting chubby," Maria uttered.

Maria had recently started dating a boy named Todd, a high school junior who attended Quigley South Boys High School in Chicago.

"He said what? You're tiny! What are you now, a size one?" Lori asked.

"I'm a size three now. Todd was trying to pick me up the other day, and he said that I was too heavy for him to carry," Maria explained.

"That's ridiculous. You're in great shape. Your body is just filling out and developing into a woman's body. You're only a size three for Christ's sake," Tanisha groaned.

"Tanisha, don't use the Lord's name in vain," Lori scolded gently.

"Sorry, Lori," Tanisha offered.

"I know. But he wants me to be a size one," Maria defended.

"Well, you're a good size now. If you're trying to lose weight for you, that's one thing, but don't lose weight for no man!" Tanisha challenged. She often used incorrect grammar or spoke Ebonics to emphasize a point.

Tanisha took a sip from her chocolate milk before continuing. "And don't go starving yourself into a skeleton like those scrawny white girls on the cheerleading squad with you. Remember our motto: Black girls eat. White girls don't. Besides, nobody wants a bone except a dog."

"Amen, Tanisha. You're a great size, Maria," Lori echoed. "I wish I was the size you are now."

"I agree," Rashanda added. "I weigh as much as you do, Maria and I'm trying to gain a few pounds. I don't like being super skinny."

Maria giggled, "You're probably right. My mom is worried about me because I've not been eating dinner and I usually skip breakfast. Rashanda, I'll eat the rest of your cookies if you don't want them."

"You go, girl. We won't let you blow up like the Goodyear Blimp, but you can eat a meal," Tanisha said.

"For real! I'm gonna say something to that Todd the next time I see him. He has a lot of nerve telling you you're getting heavy, as tiny as you are! Last time I saw him, he didn't look like a swimsuit model!" Lori teased.

"I know. He has a little gut and never works out, but he always has something to say about how I look. I'm going to say something to him myself," Maria said.

The other girls knew that Maria would not confront Todd about his comments just like she didn't confront him when he said that her nose looked like a bird's beak.

BRRRRRRiinng!! The bell rang signaling the end of the lunch period, so the girls threw away their trash and scooted off to class.

When Tanisha got home from school that afternoon, Billie Mae was sitting in the living room painting her nails a bright orange color. The night before, Tanisha had fallen asleep before Billie made it home from her Buddhist meeting.

"Hi, mom. I tried to pay half of the phone bill yesterday, but they wanted all of it since the phone was turned off," Tanisha cleared her throat. "But since the house was already wired for two lines they let me get a phone in my name since there's a jack in my room upstairs, so it didn't cost extra. Here's the number that they gave me." Tanisha handed Billie the piece of paper and held her breath, bracing herself for Billie's explosion.

"Put it on the table. My nails are wet. I'm going to get my phone turned back on when I feel like it." Billie blew on her nails. "But in the meantime, I'll use your phone when I need to use the phone."

Tanisha exhaled, gathered her backpack and walked slowly to her room to study.

Please, God! Help me score a sixteen hundred on my SAT so I can get a scholarship and escape this house of horror.

She plopped on the floor and leaned her back against the metal bed frame to start her homework. She fumbled in her backpack and pulled out her notebook and pencil. The pencil rolled under the bed. Her hand patted under the bed, and she froze as her hand felt cloth.

She tugged slightly and stared at the tattered towel, a terry cloth reminder of her secret shame.

Chapter 7

More to the Story

Tanisha was a bed wetter. Until she was almost eleven years old, she awakened to wet sheets at least four or five times each week. She'd tried everything to control her bladder. She stopped drinking liquids after six o'clock and set an alarm clock by her bed to awaken her at midnight to use the bathroom only to change her soaked pajamas. Nothing worked.

She slept on the same thin mattress that she'd had when she was a toddler sleeping on the bottom bunk while Jack snored loudly on the top bunk. As Tanisha grew and the bed wetting continued, urine slowly corroded the cheap mattress material and began to rust the mattress springs which poked through, scraping her legs and thighs.

As a second grade bed wetter, she felt responsible for her condition and was too ashamed to ask for help. Her brothers had stopped wetting the bed as toddlers. Her pride would not allow her to highlight her condition with her parents, so she hid it. She washed her sheets and stuffed the hole in her mattress. When they moved to Newberry East from Chicago, Tanisha carefully placed fitted sheets on both sides of her mattress so no one noticed the large hole in the center. She learned to sleep on a towel to absorb some of the urine and to pad the hole for comfort. Each morning Tanisha hung the urine soaked towel in her closet to dry and washed the towel with her weekly laundry. As the years progressed, the hole grew larger and larger. Tanisha stuffed the hole with rags and old towels.

She hadn't wet the bed in over three years, but her mattress was a daily reminder of her bed wetting shame. Tanisha sighed loudly and stuffed the rag back into the hole. *Every time I plan to talk to Daddy or Billie about needing a new mattress, a new family crisis crops up that involves money, and I lose my nerve. They have enough on their plate as it is.* She pulled out her algebra book and started her homework.

The next afternoon, Tanisha gave herself a pep talk in anticipation of asking Darrell to the Turnabout dance. She'd role played what she would say with Lori, Maria and Rashanda over lunch and they had coached her on what to do.

"When you ask him, I think you should stand really close to him so that you can smell his breath. You should be close enough to kiss him when you talk to him," Maria advised.

"What? You're tripping. Why would she want to be all in his face?" Lori asked.

"Men like it when their woman is up close and personal," Maria explained.

"Well, first of all, I'm not his woman," Tanisha corrected.

Maria and Lori echoed simultaneously. "Not yet!"

"Jinx you owe me a Snickers!" Maria pointed her finger at Lori.

"Besides, what if my breath is tart?" Tanisha asked. "I don't want to blow stank breath in his face when I talk to him."

"Good point. Here, Tanisha," Rashanda agreed. "Why don't you take the entire peppermint today and pop it in your mouth just before you go to pom pon." Rashanda handed Tanisha a starlight mint.

Rashanda's mom always packed one peppermint or butterscotch hard candy in her lunch. The four girls had Humanities class right after lunch. Humanities was a combination English and literature class that spanned two class periods and was reserved for Honors students. Every day in Humanities class, Rashanda would crack the peppermint in the plastic wrapper by crushing it between her braces. The girls followed an honor system to assign the largest piece of peppermint. The crew looked forward to the peppermint treat. But all were more than happy to forego the small sweet for the cause of helping Tanisha's breath remain fresh for her Darrell encounter. Tanisha tucked the peppermint star into the pocket of her jeans.

After algebra class, Tanisha raced to the restroom to smooth out her hair and apply more lip gloss. She also remembered to pop the peppermint star in her mouth. She ran to her locker to get her jacket and backpack and headed to the gymnasium.

As Tanisha chewed the last bit of the peppermint candy, she saw Darrell approaching the doors to the gymnasium. Darrell was wearing Tanisha's favorite red and blue striped rugby shirt and his Calvin Klein jeans.

He has such a cute butt! Darrell Hunter had been the inspiration for Tanisha to get a pair of Calvin Klein jeans. *Okay, don't be nervous. You know what his answer is, just go ahead and ask him.*

Her heart raced with anticipation, but she was anxious to get this over with. *If I walk a little bit faster, I can meet him at the door so I won't have to call his name.*

Tanisha picked up her pace and increased her stride so that she arrived at the gymnasium door just as Darrell was placing his hand on the handle. He looked up and held the door open for Tanisha.

"Hey, Tanisha. After you." Darrell smiled widely showing his mouth full of braces. Darrell and Rashanda were patients of Dr. Pavlicka and had gotten braces within two weeks of each other.

"Thanks, Darrell. Chivalry isn't dead after all," Tanisha replied coyly.

"It's my pleasure, Miss Carlson. Nice jeans," Darrell noticed. "I haven't seen you in a few days."

"Thanks. Your loss," Tanisha said playfully.

"Oh, is that right? What did I lose?" Darrell played along.

"You missed the opportunity to see me every day!" Tanisha was glad that Rashanda had given her that peppermint. She'd had chili for lunch and could smell the ground beef on her tongue.

"So I hear you want to ask me something." Darrell was smiling at Tanisha as he moved within twelve inches of her.

Maria was right. Boys do like invading your personal space. "You know what I want to ask you. So is it yeah or nay?" Tanisha teased. She arched her eyebrow curiously. His breath smelled like he needed a peppermint.

"I don't know. You haven't asked me anything yet," Darrell grinned.

"You're going to make me say it. Okay, fine I'll say it. Do you have any gum?" Tanisha joked.

"Gum? Do I have any gum?" Darrell replied with a puzzled look.

"I'm kidding. Do you want to go to Turnabout with me?" Tanisha was now nervous again and spit it out before she lost her nerve.

"Well, do you want to go with me?" Darrell was teasing again.

"What do you think?" Tanisha could see the clock over Darrell's left shoulder and noted that she had five minutes to change into her gym uniform or she would be marked tardy for pom pon rehearsal. Anyone who arrived for pom pon practice after the teacher was marked tardy and had to stay behind and clean up the pom pon rehearsal area which meant sweeping all of the stray pom pons.

"A little bird told me that you did." Darrell flashed his wire smile again.

"Well, your little bird was right. So is that a yes?" Tanisha was enjoying his playful teasing but had to hurry him along. If she got stuck cleaning the pom pon area, she might miss the last activity bus back to Cedar Grove. If she missed the bus, she would have to call Billie to pick her up, and Tanisha was not in the mood for a Billie encounter today.

"Sure. It would be fun. CJ and Lori are going so we can hang out with them," Darrell responded.

"Okay. I'll write down my number so we can coordinate the details." Tanisha grabbed her notebook from her backpack and quickly scribbled her number down and handed it to him.

"Hunter! Are you joining the basketball practice or are you trying out for cheerleading?" Coach Green walked up just as Tanisha handed Darrell her phone number.

"I'm getting changed right now, Coach." Darrell smiled at Tanisha. He extended his pinky and thumb in opposite directions creating the formation of a telephone and placed it to his ear to signal that he would call her later. He winked and scurried down the stairs to the boys' locker room.

Tanisha raced to the girls' locker room, pulled her gym uniform out of her gym basket and changed in ninety seconds. As she changed, her thoughts wandered to Byron Bird. She thought that Darrell was cute, and looked forward to going to her first dance with him, but he didn't make her heart pitter patter the way that Byron Bird did. She longed to see Byron again.

She placed her gym basket back into its slot and sprinted to the upper deck of the gymnasium a mere ten seconds before the teacher arrived, saving her from pom pon clean up duties.

"Girl, you made it. That was close! I saw you down there talking to Darrell," Lori whispered. "I was afraid you were going to be late!"

"Me too," she huffed. "That was close, but I made it!" Tanisha took a deep breath and rolled the fabric of her gym uniform to just below her buttocks, a style that most of the girls adopted in an effort to add a sense of flair to the drab uniform and display their legs for the boys in the gym.

"You can tell me how your chat with Darrell went on the activity bus after practice," Lori said. She pointed to a fresh scar on Tanisha's leg. "What happened to your thigh?" The scratch measured about one inch in length.

Tanisha rubbed the scratch. "Oh this? I scratched myself with the staple in my folder. I was doing homework in shorts and ran my folder across my thigh."

"You're always bruising yourself. You had a similar scratch last week on your other thigh," Lori reminded.

Tanisha stood up and slowly rolled up her other gym short leg and got in line in front of Lori to begin rehearsals, as the teacher put on the cassette of Earth Wind and Fire's *Got to Get You Into My Life*.

"I know. I have to stop buying these cheap folders with the staples that hang out. I need to put some cocoa butter on this one." Tanisha continued to rub the scratch and made a mental note to stuff another towel in the hole. She was running out of excuses to explain the scrapes on her legs. It was time for a new mattress.

Chapter 8

She Works Hard for the Money

"Who do you think you are? We don't have groceries, and you're going on a ski trip? You have a lot of nerve little girl," Billie snarled. It was Friday and Billie was driving Tanisha to her part-time job at Save Mart.

"I didn't know it was my responsibility to buy groceries," Tanisha mumbled.

"What did you say? I know you're not back talking me. Girl, I will pull this car over and smack the taste out of your mouth!" Billie guided the car with her left hand while her cigarette dangled between her right index and middle finger. "You think because you have a little job now that you're grown. Well, you're not grown. I have half a mind not to sign that damn permission slip." Billie spat the words out of her mouth.

Tanisha sat quietly. She didn't have time to have her dad sign the permission slip since she had to give it to Leslie by Sunday night along with the trip fee. "It's not like you're paying for it. It's my money and if I want to spend it on a ski trip, then I don't see what the big deal is," Tanisha argued.

Tanisha had been invited to a John & Judy ski trip in Lake Geneva, Wisconsin. Her friend Leslie had invited her and Vicky to the annual ski trip that was shared by the Chicago and South Suburban John & Judy chapters. Tanisha knew that she stood a great chance of seeing Byron Bird. She had to go whatever the cost. She just had to go. The fifty five dollar trip fee was more than half of her weekly salary from her new part time job at Save Mart. Vicky also worked at Save Mart and had encouraged Tanisha to apply. Tanisha recalled the conversation vividly.

"*Tanisha, you're tall and you're mature for fourteen. Plus, with all of the honors classes that you're taking, they'll believe that you're fifteen,*" *Vicky encouraged.*

"*What if I get busted?*" *Tanisha asked.*

"*You won't. Trust me. The personnel director's name is Denise Lemke. Just tell her that you're a classmate of mine. Denise loves me. Make sure you bring a copy of your report card so she can see that you're a straight A student. Just white out anything that has your grade on it. She knows that Battle Creek Junior High School goes through ninth grade so she'll believe that you're a freshman once she sees all of the freshman classes that are on your schedule,*" *Vicky coached.*

"*I'm scared, but I really need this job,*" *Tanisha shared.*

"*Girl, Denise is really cool. Once she meets you, she'll love you. Don't forget to tell her that your parents are divorced. That way she can hire you through the work program for fifteen year olds,*" *Vicky explained.* "*And remember to wear make-up and dress nice so you look a little older.*"

"*Got it.*" *Tanisha dressed in her nicest sweater and corduroys and had Jack drive her to Save Mart. Tanisha completed the application neatly and met briefly with Denise. Although she was very nervous, she felt that she'd left a good impression. Not a great first impression, but a good one.*

She was surprised when she received a call the following Friday with a job offer as a cashier. The pay rate was three dollars and thirty five cents an hour which was the minimum wage, but it was two dollars and thirty five cents more per hour than she made babysitting. Tanisha started cashier training the following Saturday. Six weeks into her part-time job, she was given checkout supervisor responsibilities.

Billie gripped the steering wheel with her left hand and tapped her cigarette into the full ashtray with her right hand. Tanisha could tell that Billie was furious with her. Billie started chanting her Buddhist prayer and breathing deeply.

"Nam yo ho ringe ko. Nam yo ho ringe ko," Billie hummed loudly. Tanisha wanted to jump out of the car. *Just four more blocks, and we'll be at Save Mart.* Billie had become obsessed with Buddhism. She was convinced that if she recited this Buddhism chant, left money and fruit on her Buddhist altar, and attended regular meetings that Buddha would bring prosperity and peace into her life. As far as Tanisha could tell, it wasn't working.

Tanisha and her siblings were often awakened by Billie performing her morning Buddhist chant and ringing her gong. Billie Mae had recently quit her administrative job at the college and was usually too busy attending Buddhism meetings to take Tanisha to her part-time job so most days Tanisha had to ride her bike to and from work since the bus didn't travel down the rural streets where the Save Mart was located.

Save Mart was only about a mile and a half from her house in a town called Steiffer, but the road that she had to take to get there was without street lights for about half a mile. Tanisha was afraid of the dark road when she rode her bike and prayed for safe travels to and from. Occasionally, an older female colleague named Mary Ellen would place her bike in her station wagon and give her a ride home after closing because she didn't want Tanisha riding home in the dark. Tanisha knew that it was dangerous to ride at night, but she had no choice. She couldn't afford to take taxis too often and she needed the money from her job at Save Mart. She'd already saved over four hundred dollars in the three months that she'd started working part-time.

Every week Billie made Tanisha contribute seven dollars to the household. If Tanisha didn't immediately give Billie the seven dollars each Friday, Billie would ask for it. Billie knew that Tanisha got paid on Fridays and was paid in cash, so she generally made herself available to take Tanisha to work on Fridays so that she could collect her seven dollars and buy a pack of cigarettes and a pint of beer. Tanisha called Billie the beer drinking Buddhist. *Aren't Buddhists supposed to denounce alcohol and cigarettes?*

Billie pulled the car into the Save Mart parking lot. "I need you to go inside and get your check so you can give me my seven dollars, Tanisha."

"But it's time for me to punch in. I don't have time to get my check and come back outside. I'll be late for work! Can't I just give it to you tonight?" Tanisha asked.

"I need my money now." Billie steered the Chrysler New Yorker parallel to the front window of the store and put the car in park. "Go get my money, and I'll sign your permission slip for that stupid ski trip."

Tanisha was mortified. She had four minutes to run to the back of the store, place her purse in her locker, put on her teal smock, swipe in and get to the checkouts to start her shift. But she knew that Billie would come into the store and make a scene if she didn't pick up her pay envelope and give Billie her money.

Tanisha jumped out of the car and raced to the cash cage at the back of the store to pick up her check. She was in luck. There was only one person ahead of her so she got her check in less than one minute. She then raced to her locker, put on her smock, threw her pay envelope into the pocket of her smock and punched in. She swiped her time clock with one minute to spare.

Tanisha raced to the front of the store just as Mary Ellen was checking her watch.

"I'm sorry I'm late, Mary Ellen," Tanisha explained.

"I was beginning to worry. I have to punch out now so I don't get an overtime charge. Let me go over the checkout activity real fast!" she said. "Kathy is on break. Sue needs to go to lunch when Kathy gets back and Donna is coming at six o'clock. Security wants you to look out for a woman with a baby stroller and make sure she pays for a pair of earrings..." Mary Ellen continued to give Tanisha the checkout supervisor update when Tanisha saw Billie approaching the checkouts. Tanisha's jaw fell open.

Following Tanisha's gaze, Mary Ellen stopped talking and stared at Billie.

"Where's my money, Tanisha?" Billie asked gruffly.

"Excuse me, Mary Ellen." Tanisha turned to face her mother. "I was going to bring it out to you in a minute. It's in my pocket," Tanisha whispered. She prayed that she had the exact amount in her pay envelope or she would have to give Billie more than the seven dollars. If that happened, she could cancel any hope of getting any change back. She reached in her smock pocket and ripped open her pay envelope. With overtime, her pay for that week was one hundred thirty four dollars and ten cents. Save Mart paid its employees in cash with the thought that employees would be more likely to shop in the store if they didn't have to leave the store to cash their check. Tanisha didn't have exact change and would have to give Billie a ten dollar bill. As Tanisha was about to hand Billie the ten dollar bill, Mary Ellen interrupted.

"Do you need change, Tanisha? I can give you change from the cash drawer."

"Yes. Thanks, Mary Ellen. I just need a five and five singles," Tanisha said.

Mary Ellen had seen Billie come into the store on more than one occasion and take money from Tanisha. Tanisha handed Billie a five and two singles. Billie snatched the money from her, rolled her eyes at Mary Ellen and left the store.

Mary Ellen winked at Tanisha and continued with her checkout supervisor update. "Why don't you go and lock your pay stub in your locker so you don't get in trouble," she advised.

The cashiers and checkout supervisors were forbidden from keeping more than twenty dollars in their smock pocket.

"Are you sure? You'll punch out late if I do that," Tanisha reminded.

"That's okay. I haven't punched out late all week so five minutes won't hurt my timesheet. Now scoot, kiddo!" Mary Ellen winked at Tanisha and gently nudged her shoulder.

Tanisha raced to the back of the store to lock her money away. She liked Mary Ellen's style.

Chapter 9

Frigid Friends

The snow fell in a steady stream, covering the sleeping brown grass like a fluffy white down comforter. In typical Midwest fashion, the past weekend's temperatures had reached a high of fifty degrees Fahrenheit. The promise of spring was in the air. The heavy winter coats were temporarily replaced by sweaters and sweatshirts as the outer layer. Loafers were slipped on without socks, and gloves and mittens were tossed into the back of the closet where they would soon mingle with moth balls and cedar chips.

Days later, the brief March thaw was followed by temperatures in the low thirties. The weatherman predicted six inches of snow for most of the Chicago area. The village of Newberry East was under a severe storm watch and falling temperatures through the night.

Tanisha loved winter and snow. She loved everything about the snow: its texture, taste and the look of freshly fallen white snowflakes. She loved how snow whispered its way into the world unlike rain which was noisy and loud. Snow was quiet. Snow didn't mess up your hair the way that rain did. If you wore a nice wool hat in the snow, you could cover and protect your hairstyle. You might get a few snowflakes on any exposed hair, but you could shake those out. With rain, once your hair got wet, the style was washed away. No, Tanisha definitely preferred snow to rain. She sometimes sneaked and ate snow, enjoying the cool feel on her tongue and chewing the clumps like cold cotton candy.

The John & Judy ski trip was only one week away and Tanisha was excited about the prospect of seeing Byron. She wasn't sure if he'd be on the ski trip, but she knew there was a strong possibility that he might be since the South Suburban Chapter and the Chicago Chapter sponsored the trip together. Tanisha borrowed a ski bib from her cousin so she could look the part of a real skier. Maria had also been invited to the John & Judy ski trip by a friend who was a member of John & Judy. Tanisha and Maria were on the phone doing their algebra homework together and comparing their answers.

"I'm so excited that the ski trip is only one week away! Are you going to ski, Tanisha?" Maria squealed.

"I'm going to try. I've never skied before. Are you skiing?" Tanisha asked.

"No. I'm going to go horseback riding," Maria replied.

"Oh. That sounds like fun. Leslie and Vicky are going horseback riding too. I hope I don't hurt myself skiing, but I want to give it a try. My cousins are all skiers so hopefully it's in my genes, and I can learn quickly," Tanisha said. She chewed on her pencil and studied the next algebra problem.

"You're athletic, so it shouldn't be a problem for you," Maria encouraged. There was a slight pause before she continued. "Tanisha, I feel like I need to tell you something," Maria said slowly.

"What's up?" Tanisha switched the phone from her left hand to her right, and twirled the phone cord in her hand.

"You know that guy Byron Bird you met a few months ago?" Maria asked.

"What about him?" Tanisha held her breath.

"My friend Gina told me that Byron already has a girlfriend. She said that he is going with this girl named Rebecca from the Chicago chapter of John & Judy," Maria finished.

Tanisha's heart skipped a bit. *That explains why Byron hasn't called. He has a girlfriend!* Tanisha had never considered that he might have a girlfriend. *Why did he ask for my phone number if he has a girlfriend?* Tanisha was confused.

"I just thought you should know in case you saw them together on the ski trip. I hope you're not mad at me for telling you," Maria said.

Tanisha had to regroup. "Thanks, Maria. I appreciate you looking out for me. That explains why he never called. Oh well, life goes on. I'm over him now anyway," she lied. "I'm not surprised by this. All along I figured that if he'd lost my number and really wanted to reach me he could have gotten my phone number from Leslie."

Tanisha bit into her pencil and felt her stomach churn. "I'm almost done with problem number six. Did you get six xy for an answer?" she asked.

"Yeah, I did. Wow! You're handling this very well. I'd be pissed if I found out a boy I liked already had a girlfriend. I'm working on problem number seven now. I'm glad we can do our homework together, Tanisha," Maria continued.

"Me, too. It helps to check it with you before we face Ms. James," Tanisha agreed. "By the way, have you lost more weight?" Tanisha asked.

"Can you tell? I've lost five more pounds. I weigh one hundred and two now, but I really want to weigh ninety five pounds. Todd still thinks that I'm chubby," Maria groaned.

"Maria, for the umpteenth time, you're not chubby," Tanisha repeated.

Maria had stopped eating lunch entirely. She would sip her chocolate milk and play with her food always complaining that something was wrong with her meal. Tanisha hadn't really paid attention to her lack of eating during lunch but had begun to notice that her designer jeans were fitting a lot looser. At five feet four inches tall, Maria was a slight build with long legs and narrow hips and her recent weight loss made her look sickly.

"Maria, we're worried about you. Todd is starting to make you feel bad about yourself. You were a good size before, but now you look sickly, and we never see you eat," Tanisha scolded.

"That's not true. I eat at home. I'm just not really hungry at lunchtime," Maria explained. Her voice was shrill and defensive.

"Well, I don't want you to get so wrapped up in what Todd thinks that you lose sight of what you think. I think you look great. Personally, I think he has too much control over you and Lori agrees," Tanisha continued.

"Oh, since when do you and Lori sit around talking about me? Huh? Todd loves me and wants what's best for me. If you were my friend, you would be happy for me!" Maria screamed into the phone.

"Maria, I am your friend, but I don't want to watch him mess up your head. Calm down. Don't get mad at me, we're just worried about you," Tanisha said.

"Whatever! I think you're just jealous because I have a better body than you do, and I have a boyfriend! You're just trying to make me feel bad because I told you that Byron has a girlfriend! That's pretty low, Tanisha!" Maria slammed the phone down.

Tanisha couldn't believe it. She and Maria had gotten closer over the year, and she couldn't believe that Maria would interpret her concern for envy. She needed another opinion. She dialed Lori and prayed that her sister Charlotte wasn't on the phone.

"Hello." Lori answered on the second ring.

"Hey girl, it's Tanisha. I'm so glad you answered the phone."

"Hey, Tanisha," Lori whispered. "As usual, I'm sitting here guarding the phone from Charlotte because I'm expecting a call from CJ so we can talk about what we're wearing to the dance. What's up?"

"Girl, Maria just went off on me and hung up!" Tanisha shrieked.

"What happened?" Lori asked.

"We were doing our algebra homework and she told me that Byron Bird had a girlfriend who was in the Chicago Chapter of John & Judy. Her name is Rebecca, and she is going to be on the ski trip. Maria didn't want me to bump into him with his girlfriend and be crushed since she knows how I was looking forward to seeing him to find out why he never called."

"That was nice of her. Because it would have knocked the wind out of you if you had just bumped into them holding hands or something," Lori agreed.

"I guess you're right. I'm glad that she clued me in about Byron," she admitted. "At least now I won't be stunned if I see him with a girl. Anyway, I thought that since we were looking out for each other, I would take the opportunity to tell her that I thought that she was getting too thin," Tanisha continued sincerely. "She told me that she weighs one hundred and two pounds, and she is trying to lose about seven more."

"You're kidding. Rashanda only weighs about one hundred and five pounds, and we all agree that she's too skinny," Lori reminded.

"Exactly. So I told her that we were worried about her and that she shouldn't let Todd influence how she feels about herself. You know the stuff we talked about."

"Right. What'd she say?" Lori asked.

Tanisha pushed her algebra homework to the side and stretched her legs. "She was pissed that we'd been discussing her behind her back."

"Did you use my name?" Lori asked.

"Of course. I told her that we were her friends and that we were worried about her."

"What else did she say?" Lori quizzed.

"She flipped out. She said that I was jealous of her because she has a better body than I do. She accused me of just being angry for telling me that Byron has a girlfriend and that I just wanted to make her feel bad. She also said that Todd loved her and that I was just mad because I didn't have a boyfriend," Tanisha finished.

"Wow. She went off on you," Lori whistled into the phone.

"I know. I was just trying to be a friend and she went off the deep end. I think you should call her, Lori," Tanisha encouraged.

"Why should I call her? What would I say? I don't want her going off on me," Lori whined.

"You know she knows that I called you right away. Just call her and tell her that you're also worried about her and see what happens," Tanisha coached.

"Okay, I'll call her right now and call you back. Don't get on the phone!" Lori instructed.

Tanisha decided to finish her algebra homework. She was tempted to call Rashanda but she didn't have call waiting and didn't want the phone to ring busy when Lori called back. Fortunately, Billie Mae had gotten her phone line turned back on the previous week so Tanisha didn't have to worry about anyone else wanting to use the phone.

Her thoughts drifted to the upcoming spring dance. Darrell and Tanisha had agreed that they would wear tan and yellow to the Turnabout. Tanisha had a pretty yellow sun dress that would be perfect. She hoped that the temperatures would warm up for the April dance. Since Tanisha had asked Darrell to be her date, they'd spoken on the phone twice. She liked Darrell, and was excited to be going to her first dance, but Darrell didn't make her heart leap. She finished another algebra problem as the phone rang.

Tanisha grabbed it on the first ring. "Hellooooo." Tanisha loved dragging out the o in hello. She called it her sultry adult voice. It was Lori.

"She went off on me too, Tanisha. She's a trip!" Lori exclaimed.

"What happened?" Tanisha asked excitedly.

"She told me that her weight was none of my business, and that if I were really her friend that I would stay out of it and be happy that she found a man that loves her," Lori stated.

Tanisha was relieved that Lori hadn't experienced better treatment than she'd received from Maria.

"What do you think we should do now?" Tanisha asked. She idly stared out the window watching the snow cover everything in sight.

"There's not much else we can do. We told her that we were worried about her and she told us to back off," Lori said. "It's out of our hands."

"True. But we can't just leave it at that." Tanisha pressed her nose to the window pane and blew. She wrote her initials in the steam that her breath created. "I'd like to talk to her mother so her mother can talk some sense into her, but I'm afraid Maria would view that as betrayal," Tanisha admitted.

"I agree. I mean we can't really get to her mother without her knowing about it. But you would think that her mother is noticing how skinny Maria is getting," Lori suggested.

"I know, but now that her mother is back in school, she's not home as much. We need to get Todd out of her life or at least get him out of her head so deep," Tanisha decided.

"I agree, but how are we going to do that?" Lori asked.

"I don't know," Tanisha said softly. *But Todd is clearly the problem and we have to eliminate the problem before our friend Maria spins out of control.*

Chapter 10

Coy Boy

Just days before the John & Judy ski trip, the tension in the hallways of Battle Creek Junior High was as thick as a London fog. Maria ostracized herself from Tanisha and Lori. She continued to sit next to the girls at lunch but only spoke to them if she were asked a direct question. She was gay and fun with Rashanda whom she didn't view as a traitor. Although Rashanda was just as culpable as Tanisha and Lori and had made the same observations and comments about Maria's weight, Rashanda hadn't verbalized them to Maria.

In an effort to get the friendship rhythm back on track, Tanisha and Lori apologized to Maria by saying that they only had her best interest at heart and that if she were happy with Todd then they were happy for her. But nonetheless, Maria wouldn't budge. She remained convinced that Tanisha and Lori had a conspiracy going and were out to destroy her personal happiness.

The Friday of the ski trip departure, Tanisha packed her weekend bag and walked the short block to Leslie's house so that she could ride with Leslie and Vicky to Homer Glen High School where the charter bus would take the group to the ski lodge in Lake Geneva, Wisconsin. Billie Mae was at a Buddhist meeting when Tanisha left. Tanisha was glad that Billie wasn't home. Although she'd reluctantly signed the permission slip, Billie was not pleased that Tanisha was going on this trip.

Tanisha sat next to Vicky on the charter bus and listened to her friend's story about her newest boyfriend. When Vicky finished,

Tanisha quietly confided to Vicky that she'd met a boy who went to HG high school, but he'd never called her and she hoped that she would see him on the ski trip. She also shared with Vicky that she'd just found out that he had a girlfriend. Tanisha had scarcely finished her story before Vicky leaned back to take a nap. Tanisha settled into her seat and stared out the window.

She leaned her head against the cold glass and dozed. She was startled when her head banged against the glass pane as the bus drove over a speed bump. She stretched her arms and looked out the window.

The same winter storm watch that had hit Chicago earlier in the week had hit Wisconsin. The resort resembled a postcard. The treetops glistened with snow and icicles from the frigid temperatures. Tanisha recognized two Clydesdale horses from Budweiser commercials, pulling a large open air sleigh through the snow. The guests on the sleigh huddled under heavy wool blankets for warmth. Tanisha stretched her arms, and pulled out her mirror to freshen up. *I might run into Byron in the lobby, and I don't want my hair to be flat when I see him.*

Once inside, the ski lodge was just as Tanisha imagined. There were two fireplaces with overstuffed sofas and chairs. The knotty pine furniture was well worn and looked very comfortable. Large deer antlers hung over one of the fireplaces while stuffed mallards and a moose head hung over the second fireplace. A black bear skin rug lay in front of the fireplace. Tanisha wondered if it was real.

The registration process went smoothly and the girls headed to their hotel room to freshen up and change for dinner. As they walked to dinner, Tanisha spotted Byron Bird from across the room. It had been over three months since she'd met him and he appeared to be at least an inch taller, and as handsome as she remembered. Her heart skipped a beat. Tanisha pointed him out to Vicky.

"You're right, Tanisha. He is cute. You should go over and say hi to him," Vicky encouraged.

"What if he doesn't remember me?" Tanisha's heart raced.

"What are you talking about? Of course he'll remember you," Vicky said.

Tanisha wasn't so sure. He had asked for her phone number and had never used it. Plus, he had a girlfriend. So maybe she hadn't made the impression on him that she'd thought.

"Will you come with me?" Tanisha pleaded.

Vicky was a sophomore at River North and had more experience with boys than Tanisha. "Of course I will. Let's go," Vicky said confidently.

"You think we should go over there now?" Tanisha stammered.

"Why not? Let's go." Vicky grabbed Tanisha's arm and gently led her across the room.

"Okay. Stop for one second, Vicky." Tanisha popped a wintergreen tic tac in her mouth and chewed it vigorously. Tanisha's insides were quivering, but she had to speak with him. She had to learn why he never called her.

Byron was standing with two other guys when Tanisha walked up to him. His back was facing her and she raised her hand to tap him on the back. Vicky grabbed her hand and shook her head no. She gently pulled Tanisha back and whispered. "Just wait, Tanisha. He'll turn around in a second. Watch," Vicky assured.

As if on Vicky's cue, seconds later, one of his friends nodded his head in their direction and nudged Byron. "Hey Byron, I think they're waiting for you."

Byron turned around slowly glancing at Vicky and then smiling widely at Tanisha. Tanisha returned his smile with a wide tight lipped smile and a flirtatious tilt of her head to the left.

Tanisha had worn her new tan corduroy pants that hugged her hips nicely. She also wore a white cotton turtleneck and a tan hooded cardigan sweater with her rubber Sporto duck boots. She'd made sure to apply a little mascara and eye liner and had on light pink lipstick. Her hair was a natural reddish brown and she'd recently gotten a fresh relaxer. Since working at Save Mart part-time, Tanisha had been able to enhance her wardrobe with some key pieces and had started getting her hair done once per month. She'd splurged on a few nicer items for the ski trip knowing that she might see Byron.

"Hey! What's up?" Byron asked. His tone was upbeat and energetic.

"Hey Byron! Long time no see. You probably don't even remember who I am," Tanisha teased.

"I remember you. We met at Alpine Lake. You're Leslie's friend," Byron said.

Tanisha was relieved. He at least remembered her association with Leslie. "I'm Tanisha. Tanisha Carlson," she offered.

"Right. I remembered your name," Byron explained.

"Yeah, right. This is my friend Vicky," Tanisha said.

"Hi. It's nice to meet you," Vicky smiled.

"These are my friends Steve and Don," Byron replied.

Byron's friends grinned goofily at Tanisha and Vicky, ogling them like fresh meat. Their flattering stares were wasted on Vicky and Tanisha. Tanisha only had eyes for Byron. And Vicky liked older boys. Byron's friends were clearly only freshman or perhaps sophomores in high school. Nonetheless, Vicky smiled and engaged the young boys in conversation, deliberately steering them a respectful distance away from Tanisha and Byron.

"You look really nice, Tanisha. Are you skiing tomorrow?" Byron asked.

"I am. Are you?" Tanisha replied nervously.

"I plan to race snow mobiles with my friends tomorrow," Byron explained.

"Oh, that should be fun," Tanisha offered.

"Yeah. We do it every year. It's a lot of fun." Byron was looking over Tanisha's shoulder clearly distracted. She turned quickly to follow his gaze.

Tanisha's confidence was increased with her new outfit and flattering stares from Steve and Don, so she asked him the question that had been burning in her mind. "So, why didn't you ever call me?" she whispered quickly. Tanisha was proud of herself for asking the question.

She'd rehearsed what she would say with Lori the night before. Lori had encouraged her that there was no reason to beat around the bush. "Just cut to the chase and ask him why he never called," Lori coached.

"I couldn't call you because I lost your phone number," Byron explained.

Strike One. Lori had warned her that he would probably try the *"I lost your number excuse."* So Tanisha was ready with her response. "Nice try. You could have gotten my number from Leslie," she said confidently.

"I never see Leslie. She's always on North campus and I'm always on South campus. And I forgot that you knew Leslie." He flashed his pearly whites at Tanisha again. This guy was a charmer, but Tanisha wasn't falling for it.

"Likely story, because you just remembered that I was Leslie's friend two seconds ago," Tanisha offered playfully. She couldn't believe that she still had feelings for Byron after only one dance but she desperately wanted him to ask her for her number again.

"Once I saw you again I remembered that you were Leslie's friend, but when I lost your number I forgot that you knew Leslie," he said quickly. "Hey listen, I've got to go talk to my boy Todd over there. It was good seeing you. I'll see you around," Byron said quickly. And then he walked away, his pace quickening as though he were chasing someone. Without saying a word, his friends trailed behind him like soldiers following the general into battle.

Tanisha was stunned. She walked over to Vicky with big eyes and relayed the story to her.

"He was nervous that his girlfriend was going to walk up and catch him talking to you. He definitely couldn't get your number in public, Tanisha. He probably still likes you but he would really be busted if she saw him with you," Vicky explained, her eyes were soft and understanding. "You should have walked away first, Tanisha," Vicky coached. "It would have been cooler if you'd left him standing there like a tin soldier," she continued. "I always make sure that I'm in control of any and all boy chats. If I hadn't been distracted by his friends, Tweedle Dum and Tweedle Dee, I would have noticed Byron fumbling and looking around nervously, and I would have pulled you away."

Tanisha wanted to cry. She wanted to crawl into a ball and cry. "You're right," she groaned. "But I was really hoping that he would ask for my number again," Tanisha whined. "I really like him. He's so tall and cute!" She felt like she was losing the battle.

"I know, but you told me on the bus that his girlfriend would probably be here," Vicky offered softly.

"I know. But I guess in my heart I was hoping that Maria's information was inaccurate," she admitted softly. "But I guess it's true. His girlfriend is here," Tanisha sighed. She shrugged her shoulders and fidgeted with the strap of her purse. "I want to meet this Rebecca babe," Tanisha said.

Vicky draped her arm softly over Tanisha's shoulder. "If she's here, you'll probably see her. But you look great and there are some fine guys on this trip. You're going to meet somebody else in a heartbeat. Watch," Vicky encouraged. "You know my motto. Boys are like buses. If you miss one bus, another bus will be along in twenty minutes," Vicky giggled. "Just wait for the next bus!"

She smiled at her friend, grateful that Vicky was willing to share her dating experience and wisdom. Tanisha trusted Vicky's wisdom and experience. At sixteen, Vicky was a dating veteran. She knew that her friend was probably right, but Byron's rejection still made her stomach churn.

Tanisha had met and bonded with Vicky and Leslie at the Cedar Grove swimming pool two summers ago. Their parents were also divorced so when Tanisha's parents split up, Vicky and Leslie had been her sounding board and helped her feel like less of a freak by sharing their divorce stories. And since they also lived in Cedar Grove, Tanisha never felt shame about where she lived when she was around them. She liked that she had two groups of friends. It was like living in two different worlds. She had her middle school buddies, plus her older, wiser high school chums, Vicky and Leslie from Cedar Grove.

"Come on, Tanisha. We've got to find Leslie," Vicky said. As they walked through the hotel lobby, Maria sashayed past Tanisha on the arm of Todd. Walking with Todd and Maria was Byron Bird holding hands with a pretty girl swinging a large Gucci purse. *That must be Rebecca!*

The group walked past without seeming to notice Tanisha and Vicky. Rebecca and Maria were chatting and giggling like old friends! As Tanisha stood frozen in her tracks, Maria glanced over her shoulder with a flip of her hair, stared Tanisha squarely in the face and rolled her eyes, without saying a word. Tanisha's mouth hung open. She didn't know what hurt more, seeing Byron Bird holding Rebecca's hand or being ignored by her friend, Maria. She decided it was a close call, but watching Maria ignore her like a stranger registered a perfect ten on the pain meter scale. A one-two punch. A left hook, followed by a solid right jab to the jaw. It was a knockout that left her down for the count. Tanisha wanted to go home. She wanted the ski trip to be over. Her legs felt like rubber bands, and her stomach tightened into a knot. She opened her mouth to speak, but the words were stuck in her throat.

Vicky shook her head in disbelief. "I know what you're thinking, Tanisha. I can't believe that Maria would flaunt past you like that. That's a violation of every friendship rule. Let's go upstairs before you lose it," Vicky whispered. She rubbed Tanisha's back and gently steered her to the elevator.

Chapter 11

Bipolar Billie

Billie cleaned out her desk. She was glad that no one had seen her come into the office, she wasn't in the mood to talk with any of her co-workers. She didn't like them anyway. She hated being given feedback and she hated deadlines. She hated everything about work except payday.

When her boss, Kaye, told her that she needed to re-organize the supply cabinet, Billie snapped.

"I am not your damn slave, Kaye!" Billie spoke the words slowly and deliberately. "I'm tired of you telling me what to do. Why can't you organize the supply cabinet?" Billie screamed.

"Billie, your job description states that maintaining order in the supply cabinet is your responsibility," Kaye said in a soft voice. Kaye was a small impish white woman who had graciously agreed to allow Billie to work in her department after a recent episode with her last boss.

Billie's outbursts and inability to take direction were discussed at a staff meeting, and Kaye had strong suspicions that Billie might have a bipolar disorder. Kaye recognized some of the manic depressive symptoms in Billie. On days when she was displaying manic behavior, Billie spoke rapidly and had visions of grandeur, believing that she was going to start a new business venture and retire a millionaire. On these days, Billie brought in flowers for her desk and answered the phone with honey in her voice. Days later, Billie would stomp in the office, complaining about how unfair the world was to her. She would glare at Kaye with daggers in her eyes and snap at the slightest request made of her.

Kaye was all too familiar with these behaviors, having lived with them for the past twenty years. Kaye's daughter was diagnosed bipolar.

"Billie, why don't we rearrange the supply cabinet together? I'll help you," Kaye suggested softly.

"Now you think I'm too stupid to do my job and I need you looking over my shoulder? I'm a typist. I can type over one hundred words per minute with less than five errors! My skills are wasted rearranging a supply cabinet," Billie barked. "I worked for William F. Wrigley, Jr., the chewing gum millionaire. I was his personal assistant! I can't believe you're asking me to rearrange a supply cabinet. This is beneath me!" Billie's voice was loud and her hands shook.

"Sometimes we all have to do things that we feel we're overqualified to do. It's just the way things are," Kaye explained. "You're an excellent typist, Billie, but right now we need to rearrange the supply cabinet so we have room for the new supplies that are being delivered tomorrow. And I need you to help me with that. Billie, as your boss, that's a reasonable request." Kaye's tone was soft and soothing.

"Why do you always have to remind me that you're my boss? I know you're my boss. And why are you talking to me like I'm your damn child? I'm a grown woman. I have four kids! Don't talk to me like a child!" Billie said loudly. Her hands shook as she spoke.

"Billie, you seem upset. Why don't you take the rest of the afternoon off? We're pretty much done here so why don't you get some rest and come back in the morning? I'll rearrange the supply closet myself," Kaye suggested.

"Why do you talk to me like I'm a mental patient? You just want me to leave so you can snoop around my desk and meddle in my things," Billie said. Her eyes were wild and her hands shook uncontrollably.

"Billie, it looks like you need a cigarette. Why don't you take your break now? You can go downstairs and have a cigarette. In fact, why don't you grab us both a cup of coffee from the cafeteria? It's my treat." Kaye reached in her purse and extended a ten dollar bill.

"Now you expect me to fetch coffee for you? Ain't that a trip? You have a lot of nerve! I will take my break now, but you can get your own damn coffee!" Billie grabbed her purse and stormed out into the hallway.

She walked into the parking lot and drove home. She didn't report to work the next day or the day after that. Kaye called each day to check on her, but the phone went unanswered until one afternoon.

◦◦◦

"Billie?" Kaye asked. "Thank God! Are you okay? I've been so worried." Kaye spoke quickly, fearful that Billie would hang up the phone.

"This isn't Billie, this is her daughter, Tanisha," Tanisha said.

"Oh Tanisha. This is Kaye from Eden State. Is your mom home? I'm really worried about her," Kaye explained.

"I just got home from school. Isn't she at work?" Tanisha asked.

"No. In fact, she hasn't been to work in over five days. I haven't spoken with her since she left the office on a break, but I noticed today that the personal things were gone from her desk. I think she may have come in while I was at lunch today and taken her things." Kaye quickly told Tanisha about their last encounter. "So you see,

I'm really worried about her. She reminds me a lot of my daughter, and I've really been trying to work with her so she can keep this job. I know she's a single parent, and she needs this job, but if she doesn't come in soon, she's going to get fired. She has used all of her sick days and vacation time, so I can't really cover for her anymore. Once I submit the time sheets my department head will see that she's out of paid time off and she will be terminated. So it's very important that you tell her to call me as soon as possible. I'm meeting with my department head tomorrow and I might be able to get him to make an exception and not fire her. Tanisha, do you know if your mom has been taking her medication?" Kaye finished.

"Medication? I'm not aware that she takes any medication," Tanisha answered.

"Oh! I'm sorry, I just assumed that you knew. I've probably said too much. Can you please just ask your mother to call me as soon as possible?" Kaye asked.

"I'll let her know as soon as I see her." Tanisha hung up the phone and shook her head.

Tanisha was puzzled. *What type of medication is Billie supposed to be taking? And if Billie hasn't been going to work, where has she been going each day while we're at school? If she doesn't work, how are we going to be able to pay the bills?* Tanisha heard a car door slam and moments later Billie walked through the front door.

"Hey, Mom!" Tanisha smiled cautiously.

"Hello. I'm going to lay down. I'm not feeling well. Where are your brothers?"

"It's Monday so they have soccer practice. Jack is picking them up today," Tanisha said.

"That's right, I forgot. Cook those pork chops that I left out on the counter for dinner," Billie ordered. She tossed her purse on the chair and headed up the stairs.

"Okay. By the way, your boss Kaye just called. She said that you need to call her as soon as possible." Tanisha's words trailed Billie up the stairs.

Tanisha could hear Billie pause on the stairwell and come back down the stairs. "What else did she say?" Billie studied Tanisha's face curiously.

"She asked me if you had been taking your medicine. What medicine is she talking about?" Tanisha asked.

Billie slanted her eyes and glared at Tanisha. She pursed her lips and spoke slowly and deliberately. "That is my personal business. I take medication to calm my nerves sometimes. But that has nothing to do with you. That woman is too nosy for her own damn good," Billie spat.

"Kaye also mentioned that you haven't been to work in several days, and that if you didn't call her as soon as possible, you were going to get fired." Tanisha folded her arms across her chest before continuing. "She also said that she thought you'd been in and removed the personal photos and things from your desk. What's going on Mom? Have you found another job?" Tanisha asked.

The room stood still. Billie glared at Tanisha with daggers in her eyes. She pointed her finger in Tanisha's face. Tanisha could smell the nicotine on her mother's fingertip. She took a small step back.

"I do not have to answer to you, little girl! I am the damn adult in this house. If I don't feel like going to work, then I won't. How dare you ask me to explain myself to you? You are a child. Now go cook those pork chops like I told you!"

"I have to do my homework first. But I'll cook them later," Tanisha said. Her voice was barely above a whisper.

She heard Billie's bedroom door slam shut and smelled cigarette smoke wafting down the stairs. Tanisha walked quickly into the kitchen and rinsed the pork chops in the sink before sprinkling season salt and a light coating of flour on both sides of the meat. She took out a box of macaroni and cheese and a can of cream style corn to cook with the pork chops. She checked under the sink and pulled out the coffee can of bacon grease that the family used to fry meat. She washed her hands and quietly tip toed up the stairs to start her homework before her brothers came home. When she reached the top stair, she heard Billie snoring on her bed. Tanisha exhaled and walked quietly into her bedroom.

Lori hadn't been in school that day and her brother had said that she was sick with a cold. Tanisha needed to clear her head after her encounter with Billie, and decided to call Lori and tell her about the ski trip weekend.

Tanisha quickly updated Lori on her Friday night Byron and Maria encounter.

"You're kidding. Maria was not hanging out with Byron and his girlfriend and Todd! I can't believe that," Lori coughed into the phone.

"Maria rolled her eyes at me like I was the devil. But wait it gets better," Tanisha continued.

After Tanisha and Vicky found Leslie, they decided to go to an unsanctioned party in the room of one of the older John & Judy teen members, David Barton. David was the most popular boy in John & Judy. His parents were both doctors and David had received a brand new black Corvette for his sixteenth birthday. He lived in a five bedroom house in the most exclusive section of Glen and had an Olympic size swimming pool in his backyard complete with a small pool house. David was known for giving the best parties in the area.

David and Leslie were classmates and Leslie had received a personal invitation for herself and her ski trip bunnies to attend David's "By Invitation Only" party. Although not in a festive mood, Tanisha knew that she couldn't spend all weekend crying in her room. Besides, all Byron had done was ask for her phone number. They weren't dating. He'd never called. Vicky reminded her of these things to help snap her out of her Byron Bird funk. It wasn't working. She liked him and wanted him to like her back. But she'd agreed to attend the party.

She'd only brought a few outfits but Vicky and Leslie were planning to change into jeans for the party, so Tanisha went back to their hotel room to change. Fortunately, she'd just bought a brand new pair of Calvin Klein jeans and a new pink and white argyle turtleneck. She'd planned to wear the turtleneck skiing on Saturday, but thought she'd better wear it to David's party instead. She wanted to look her best and knew that since Byron and David were classmates, Byron would be there with Rebecca and Todd would be with Maria.

Tanisha was determined to reclaim her lost dignity. Her pride was wounded. Maria was supposed to be her friend. How could she be cavorting with Byron's girlfriend so casually when Maria had heard Tanisha pouring her heart out for weeks about how much she liked Byron Bird? It wasn't right. Was Maria telling Rebecca about Tanisha and how much she liked Byron? Her stomach cramps returned just thinking about this as a possibility. Tanisha had been looking forward to the ski trip hayride and had imagined herself snuggled closely with Byron under a wool blanket as the horses pulled the wagons through the Wisconsin snow. Leslie and Vicky had assured her that the "real fun" would be happening at David's party.

After a quick shower, Tanisha sprayed cologne behind her ears and on her wrists, brushed her hair, dabbed some Vaseline on her lips from the little tub that she now carried and applied a light layer of strawberry lip gloss on top for flavor. She slipped on her penny loafers and waited for Vicky and Leslie to finish getting dressed. Leslie had decided that she needed to wash her hair and re-iron her outfit and Vicky was painting her nails. Tanisha watched a rerun of the Dick Van Dyke Show, dreading another encounter with Maria and her new best friend, Rebecca.

Chapter 12

What's in a Name?

Vicky decided to take a quick nap while Leslie washed her hair. "You might want to relax and get comfortable, Tanisha," Vicky suggested. "Leslie's hair maintenance routine is quite the production. It's going to take her a minute," Vicky finished, nestling into the oversized chair, a blanket wrapped tightly across her shoulders.

Leslie's hair hung to the middle of her back. Watching Leslie expertly blow dry her mane, Tanisha amused herself wondering what it would feel like to have that much hair on your head. She studied how carefully Leslie combed the tangles from her locks. *I wonder if her hair is heavy and if it keeps her neck warm in the winter? I know it makes her hot in the summer, because she always complains about it sticking to her neck? I wonder why she doesn't just get it cut since all she does is complain about it. Leslie will think I'm a knucklehead if I ask her these weirdo questions.* The television volume was muffled by the loud blow dryer, so Tanisha casually flipped through a magazine and wondered how Vicky could sleep through the blow dryer noise.

Leslie applied her mascara and lip stick and announced that she was ready to go. It was ten thirty and Tanisha was almost too tired to go to the party, but she perked up quickly and accepted a breath mint from Vicky. "Fresh breath is next to Godliness, ladies," Vicky chirped. "You know my motto, never turn down a mint. You don't know if the giver is being polite or trying to give you a subtle hint," she giggled. "I'm being polite, you ladies have minty fresh breath already," Vicky giggled. Tanisha smiled that Vicky could awaken from a sound sleep, as chipper as a cheerleader.

The girls headed out of their hotel room and walked through the hallway headed to David's room located at the opposite end of the ski resort. The chaperones had requested that the boys and girls' hotel rooms be assigned in separate wings of the resort.

As they got closer to the boys' wing of the resort, Tanisha heard the muffled sound of dance music wafting down the hall. As they walked closer to David's room, the music grew louder and louder. Tanisha's heart raced as they approached the party. Her gut told her that she would see Byron and Rebecca and possibly Todd and Maria at the party. Tanisha exhaled slowly as Leslie knocked on the door. Leslie beamed widely when a fellow classmate pulled the door open.

"Hey, Leslie!" The doorkeeper said. "You look beautiful as always!" he grinned.

"Hey, Chuck! These are my friends Vicky and Tanisha," Leslie offered.

"Hey, Ladies! I'm Chuck! Come on in and have a good time." Chuck smiled at Tanisha and whispered in her ear as she walked past him. "Nice sweater, cutie!"

Surprised by the compliment, Tanisha offered a tight-lipped half smile, her thank you barely audible. Like a robot, she trailed Vicky into the crowded hotel room, her eyes surveying her surroundings.

The room was a suite. Two full sized beds lined one wall with a round table and four chairs in the corner. A long dresser faced the beds with a television on one end of the dresser. A mirror anchored the other end of the dresser. An archway connected the larger room to a smaller room which contained a sofa along with another television nestled in the corner of the room. The smaller room also had a small kitchenette. Leslie had already shared that David always got a suite at the ski lodge and never had a roommate. Tanisha was in awe. She'd never been in a hotel suite before and was in awe that the suite that David had to himself was twice as large as the hotel room that she shared with Vicky and Leslie. She couldn't imagine what the suite cost for one night. As she looked around the room, she noticed that there were definitely more boys than girls at the party. She could feel the eyes surveying her curiously.

"I have to go to the bathroom, Tanisha," Vicky said. "I'll be right back." Feeling a sudden chill, Tanisha nervously crossed her arms over her chest and chewed her lower lip. She was glad that she'd worn a turtleneck sweater as an arctic breeze blew past her. Glancing toward the cool breeze, the patio door was ajar, a lanky boy crouched on the floor, taking quick puffs of a cigarette and exhaling into the cold, night air.

There was a small keg of beer in the kitchenette area and a group of boys circled it as though in a football huddle. At the table in the corner where the double beds were located, another group of boys were flipping quarters into a small glass. Quarter bounce! Tanisha had heard about this game from her white classmates who attended keg parties when their parents were out of town, but she had never seen it played. She knew that the object of the game was to bounce a quarter into a shot glass. If you missed, you had to take a drink of alcohol. Usually a drinking age friend of an older sibling could be bribed to buy a keg of beer and the vacationing parents' home became party central for the night; until the neighbors called the police to break up the party.

Tanisha had never been invited to a keg party but she'd heard the stories. She'd tasted beer once when her dad left a near empty can of Budweiser on the kitchen table to turn the meat on the bar-b-que grill. She took a quick swig and nearly gagged at the frothy warm taste. She quickly drank a glass of Tang to wash the bitter taste from her mouth. Tanisha didn't understand why anyone would play a game where you had to drink beer. She thought beer was disgusting.

Most of the guests were watching the new MTV channel on the two television sets. Unsure of what to do, she stood by the bathroom door to wait for her friend. As she walked out of the bathroom, Vicky was pulled aside by a tall boy who told her that she was his black Barbie and he wanted to be her Ken. Vicky giggled and smiled and told Tanisha that she would find her later. Leslie was engaged in a conversation with Chuck the doorkeeper.

Tanisha took a look around both rooms and didn't see Byron and Rebecca or Todd and Maria. She pulled back her shoulders, took a deep breath and decided to take advantage of her new girl status. She walked confidently into the kitchen and poured herself a glass of soda. She sipped on her soda and walked slowly over to the game of quarter bounce. It was clear that the others at the party were all classmates or knew each other from John & Judy. She became self conscious as the strangers stared at her curiously. The scene reminded her of how she felt at Keith Kyals' birthday party where she could hear the girls whispering about her. She took a long sip from her cup and walked closer to the table. As Tanisha approached, a cute boy offered Tanisha his seat on the edge of the bed.

"Thanks." Tanisha accepted the seat and smiled with her perfected closed mouth smile. Her dad had recently taken her to the dentist to see about having the decayed fang removed, but the dentist cautioned against pulling the tooth and advised that the permanent tooth would eventually force the tooth out on its own, so Tanisha continued to smile with the left side of her lip curled up and the right side of her lips pressed tightly together to hide the decay.

Tanisha shifted her weight on the bed for a better view of the game.

"What's your name?" asked the cute boy who was now standing over her shoulder panting like a puppy.

"Tanisha. Tanisha Carlson." Tanisha enjoyed saying her name in stages.

Before the chivalrous teen could respond, another boy was standing in front of Tanisha with his hand extended. "Hello, Tanisha. Tanisha Carlson. My name is David. David Barton. Welcome to my party. Do I know you?"

Since Leslie had been detained at the door, Tanisha hadn't met the host. Her face flushed.

"Hi, David. I'm Tanisha Carlson," she stammered. "I'm Leslie's friend," she offered quickly. *This party is invitation only. He's going to kick me out. Where's Leslie so she can explain that I'm with her.*

"I know. I saw you come in with Leslie, and I heard your name twice. That was cute. I would have let you in even if you weren't on the guest list." David stared Tanisha squarely in the eyes and shooed the boy standing over her away with his left hand and sat next to Tanisha on the bed.

Tanisha was taken aback at how handsome David was. He had blue green eyes and thick wavy black hair. He was at least six feet tall and had cocoa brown skin. When he smiled, his dimples danced in his cheeks. She noticed a deep cleft in his chin. He looked like a model in a magazine.

"Can I get you another beer?" David offered.

"Beer? No. I'm drinking 7 Up. I don't drink beer." Tanisha could smell the beer on his breath and she also smelled Paco Rabanne cologne. Tanisha knew her men's colognes. She preferred Polo cologne on boys, but on David the Paco Rabanne smelled nice.

"Oh. You're a good girl then," David teased.

"I wouldn't say all that. I'm just not old enough to be drinking yet. Especially not at a party where there are clearly more boys than girls, and I don't know that many people here," she continued. Tanisha didn't want to offend David but she hated the smell of beer and had no desire to taste it again. "But thank you for asking."

"I can respect that. But you know me now," David continued.

"True. But I just met you. I really don't know you from a can of paint. For all I know, you could be a mass murderer," she teased. "Besides, you probably don't remember my name."

"Tanisha. Tanisha Carlson. How old are you Tanisha, Tanisha Carlson?"

She was glad that she was sitting on David's right side so that he couldn't see that her tooth was decayed.

"I'm impressed. Your memory is ten seconds long," Tanisha giggled. Looking around the room, she could see the other girls at the party huddled in a corner whispering in their direction. Tanisha was feeling bold and decided to play along with David.

"David. David Barton, I'm old enough to know that I don't have to answer your question, but since this is your party, and I don't want you to throw me out on my butt, I'll tell you. But you have to keep it a secret. I'm almost fifteen. How old are you?" she whispered.

"I'm almost seventeen." David smiled widely at Tanisha.

"I think your girlfriend's friends are over there taking notes." Tanisha's eyes shifted to the right, and she tilted her head in the same direction. "You'd better scram before your girlfriend comes back, and you get busted for talking to me too long."

David glanced to the corner where Tanisha referenced and noted three of his female classmates watching him intently.

"Those are just friends from school. I don't have a girlfriend," David said.

"Yeah right! If I had a quarter for every time I heard that one." Tanisha shook her head from side to side.

"No, I'm serious. I don't have a girlfriend." David stared squarely at Tanisha, and she could feel his breath on her face. She was glad that she'd just brushed her teeth. She shifted back a few inches almost falling off of the bed. "You're funny. Has anyone ever told you that you look like Grace Kelly?" David asked.

"Grace Kelly? Isn't that the woman from that old Alfred Hitchcock movie, *Rear Window*?" Tanisha asked.

"Yeah. That's her. You remind me of her. I love that movie. You know that movie?" David asked.

"I love Alfred Hitchcock movies, and *Rear Window* is one of my favorites. But that's a new one. I look like a blonde white woman? Now you're funny. I think we need to cut you off from the beers," Tanisha giggled.

"I mean you don't look like her, it's just that you remind me of her," he stammered. "Or maybe you remind me of Doris Day. I always get those two mixed up. Where are you from Tanisha and why haven't I ever seen you before?" David asked.

Tanisha shrugged her shoulders and responded. "I don't really get out much. I've been to a few John & Judy parties this year. I live in Newberry East, and I'll be a freshman at River North in the fall. So I'm an eighth grader at Battle Creek Junior High School now. Actually, I'll still be at BCJH next year since it goes through ninth grade. So feel free to skedaddle so you're not caught chatting with a middle school toddler at your own party," she finished.

David was interrupted by a tap on his shoulder. He turned around and stood up. "Tanisha, this is Craig. Craig this is Tanisha," he introduced. "Tanisha, please excuse me for a minute," David said as he turned to face Craig. She studied his profile. She was confused by how comfortable she felt with David. When she'd met Byron, she was so smitten with him that she'd lied and told him she was a freshman at River North because she didn't want him to know that she attended middle school. But she didn't really care with David. David wasn't anything like what she'd expected. Leslie had described him as the cutest boy at HG, so Tanisha expected him to be handsome, and he was. But he was also much nicer than she expected.

She was enjoying her chat with David, but longed for Byron to walk through the door with Rebecca so that she could size her up. She tried to picture Rebecca's face. From the quick glimpse that she'd seen of her in the hotel lobby, she seemed pretty with hair that graced her shoulders. She appeared at least three inches shorter than Tanisha with a stocky, athletic build. As far as Tanisha was concerned, she was just as cute as Rebecca and didn't see what Byron saw in Rebecca that he didn't see in her.

David sat back on the bed. "Sorry about that. Now where were we?" he smiled. "Oh, you were telling me about your middle school," he remembered. "I can totally relate. I attended Parker Junior High, and we went through ninth grade too, so I know what that's like. I used to tell people I went to HG when I was in ninth grade so I would sound more mature."

"I know what you mean. I've done that a few times myself," Tanisha smiled.

David smiled back at her, his eyes staring softly into hers. She could smell a peppermint on his breath. Feeling uncomfortable under his gaze, she dropped her eyes to the floor and fidgeted with her purse strap. "Listen. Would you like to go for a walk or something?" he asked.

"I don't think so," she declined, shaking her head. "I'd better hang around and wait for my friends. Besides, this is your party. You can't leave your own party!"

"My boy Chuck will look out for things for me. Come on, let's go for a walk. It's getting too smoky in here, and I want to get some fresh air." David stood and gently pulled Tanisha up so that she was standing less than four inches away from his face. He took her hand and led her to the door.

"But I didn't bring my jacket, and it's freezing outside." Tanisha tugged slightly on David's arm. "Besides, my friends will wonder where I went."

"I don't think your friends will miss you. Look." Tanisha looked around and saw that Leslie was now playing quarter bounce in the living quarters of the suite, and Vicky was huddled in the other part of the suite laughing and talking with the same boy that had stopped her when they walked in.

"Your friends are entertaining themselves and won't even notice that you're gone. Come on, Tanisha," David pleaded. "We don't have to go outside. We can just walk around the resort," he explained.

Before Tanisha could resist again, David had grabbed her hand and led her into the hallway stopping long enough to instruct Chuck to tell Leslie that Tanisha had gone for a walk with him. Leaving with David, Tanisha could feel the stares on her back from the other girls in the party, still wondering who she was.

They walked through the hallway toward the lobby area. There were two overstuffed sofas facing one another and a pine oak table that sat between the sofas, perpendicular to the fireplace. There was a roaring fire in the hearth, and the lobby lights had been dimmed since it was now after eleven o'clock in the evening. David plopped down on the sofa and patted the seat next to him. She slipped off her shoes and sank into the oversized sofa, sitting on her feet and crisscrossing her legs like a pretzel. He bent down and picked up her loafer, sniffing it playfully and making a face. She swatted him on his shoulder and grabbed her shoe. They started to chat.

She learned that David was on the track team, the golf team, and the tennis team. He was also an avid skier and had skied competitively since he was five years old. She also learned that his parents were both physicians and shared a small family practice office in Glen. He had one sister and one brother, and he was the youngest child.

Tanisha shared that she was also on the track team and that she had just started playing tennis. She wasn't very good but she enjoyed the game. She explained that she had three brothers and that her parents were divorcing but that she saw her dad every weekend. She was surprised at how comfortable she felt sharing information with David.

"You're a tennis player too?" David asked. "I'm a good teacher, and I can help you with your tennis game, Tanisha. I'll pick you up one day after school and we can go to my neighbor's court and play," David offered.

Where does he live that his neighbor has a private tennis court? "I really just started to play," she said. "I'm not very good."

"But I can help you get better," David brightened. "I teach the junior tennis camp each summer and am really good at teaching fundamentals. You should let me pick you up for a lesson. I love helping people improve their tennis game."

"Thanks but I'm not allowed to ride in a car with a boy until I'm fifteen and only if I'm on a double date," Tanisha replied.

"Oh," David sighed. "Well, I could come to your school and we could play at your school's courts. How about that?"

"That could work, but then how would I get home?"

"Good point. I hadn't thought about that one," David confessed, a hint of desperation in his tone. "Is there a tennis court near your house?"

Tanisha squirmed slightly in her seat and crisscrossed her legs the other way, stalling for a few seconds to ponder his question. There was a tennis court in the Cedar Grove complex, but the nets weren't in good repair and the courts were nothing more than glorified asphalt painted green to resemble a tennis court. *His neighbors have a tennis court in their backyard. What will he think of my neighborhood with its asphalt covered court?*

"Yes. But the court is in really bad shape," she admitted softly. "It's really not a court at all, more like a parking lot painted green," she paused. "But there's a tennis court near my friend Maria's house so the next time I plan to go to her house, I could call you and you could meet me at those courts," she suggested.

"That could work! When are you planning to visit your friend?" David asked excitedly.

"I don't know." Tanisha bit her bottom lip. Since she and Maria were barely speaking, she didn't know when she'd be at Maria's house. "Besides, it's too cold to play tennis, and there's still snow on the ground."

"Good point. Well, Tanisha, Tanisha Carlson, who's too young to ride in my car, can I at least ski with you tomorrow? I can give you some pointers. I'm a really good teacher," David explained.

"That's so nice of you, but I've never skied before, and I wouldn't want to spoil your fun coaching me on the bunny slope," Tanisha discouraged.

"I don't mind. The slopes up here are very icy, and I prefer skiing in Colorado or Utah this time of year, so I'd love to help you learn how to ski. I'm a great teacher, and I'll have you skiing down the green slopes in no time. Trust me," David smiled.

For some reason Tanisha did trust David. She felt very comfortable with him, almost too comfortable. Tanisha stared at David and sensed sincerity in his eyes, but she was still stinging from giving her number to Byron Bird and never getting a call. She bit her lip. Just as Tanisha was about to respond, Chuck ran up to David.

"Man, I'm glad I found you," Chuck said. "Tom just got sick and threw up all over your room!"

"Oh shit! I knew he shouldn't have been playing quarters!

That boy can not hold his liquor. Did he make it to the bathroom at least?" David shook his head and frowned. He stood up and walked toward Chuck.

"Nope! He was trying to make it outside to hurl in the snow but then he lost his balance, tripped on the coffee table and threw up all over the sofa. Not to gross you out," he directed toward Tanisha. "But it was nasty. You could see the chunks of his dinner. That ended the party right there. I didn't know if you wanted me to call housekeeping or not since I'm sure it will be a special charge if they have to come clean up at this hour," Chuck finished, and spoke directly to Tanisha. "Before I forget, Leslie told me to tell you that they would meet you in the room," Chuck winked.

"Thanks," Tanisha offered softly.

"Man, go ahead and call housekeeping right now and tell them to come as soon as possible before it stinks up the whole suite," David instructed. "I'll be right there. Just make sure everyone is out of my room!" he groaned.

David walked to Tanisha's side and reached for her hand. She held her breath as he spoke. "Tanisha, I'm sorry but I've got to get back to my room. Why don't you walk back with me so we can finish talking and I'll walk you back to your room?"

"No, that's okay. I have my key so I'll just head back now since I'm already half way there," Tanisha stammered. She dropped her hand from his and stuffed both hands in her back pockets.

"Let me at least walk you back to your room. It's late, and I insist." David's voice was firm.

"Okay," Tanisha shrugged.

They headed down the hallway toward the main lobby area to the girl's wing of the resort and pressed the elevator call button. As they waited for the elevator, David continued to apologize for the interruption.

"I really enjoyed chatting with you, and I'm sorry I have to run off," David said.

"Don't worry about it. It's almost eleven thirty, and I turn into a pumpkin at eleven fifty two anyway." Tanisha tapped her watch.

"You're too funny. I'll buy you a hot chocolate on the slopes tomorrow to make it up to you. By the way, you never got back to me on that ski lesson. But I'm just going to find you on the bunny slope and tickle you until you let me teach you how to ski." David playfully tickled Tanisha's side.

She pulled away and grabbed his hands, "I tried to slide that one by you, but nothing gets by you. Since you're going to stalk me on the slopes until I say yes, I'll let you give me a quick lesson and then you can enjoy the rest of your skiing," she agreed.

"Great. I'll meet you at the ski rental booth to help you get sized up for the right skis. I'll be there at ten o'clock sharp, okay?" David reached to tickle her again.

"Okay. I'll be the one wearing a helmet and football padding." Tanisha squirmed out of his reach. "By the way, you never explained why I remind you of Grace Kelly or Doris Day," she stated.

David shrugged his shoulders. "It's something about the way that you carry yourself. I can't really explain it. It's like you're spunky and cute but not too cute but just cute enough."

Tanisha raised her eyebrows. "Not too cute, but just cute enough? What does that mean?"

"It's a compliment," David explained quickly.

"It is? That's like saying that someone's breath smells a little bad," Tanisha giggled.

David laughed at Tanisha's joke and reached to tickle her again. She squeezed his hands and pulled away as the elevator doors opened and Byron Bird stepped off.

Tanisha's expression changed when she saw Byron, and she quickly dropped David's hands. David followed her gaze.

"Hey! What's up man?! You missed my party." David gave Byron a high five.

"Yeah! You know how it is. I had some business to tend to with Rebecca." Byron let out a deep guttural laugh and David high fived Byron again. "It looks like you're headed to take care of some business of your own," Byron winked at David and stared at Tanisha.

"Naw, man, it ain't even like that. This is Tanisha," David offered.

"Yeah, we know each other. How you doing, Tanisha?" Byron smiled knowingly.

"Hi," Tanisha whispered. David studied Tanisha's facial expression.

"Well, man, I'll let you go handle yo' business!" Byron said playfully.

"All right, B. I'll see you tomorrow," David said.

David and Tanisha entered the elevator, and Tanisha pressed the button for the fourth floor.

"So how do you know Byron?" David asked quickly. He could sense that Tanisha's playfulness had worn off.

She shrugged. "I don't know him that well. I met him a few months ago at a John & Judy party." Tanisha stared at the elevator numbers wondering if it were possible for the elevator to go any slower.

"Oh. He acted like he knew you pretty well. Did he get your number?" David asked.

"Excuse me. Why does that matter?" Tanisha was startled by David's question.

"I just want to know. I've known Byron since third grade, and I'm sure he would have pushed up on you." David stared at Tanisha's profile.

The elevator was now on the second floor.

"Well, he got my number but he never called," Tanisha said. Her eyes were locked on the elevator floor numbers.

"You say that like you wanted him to call," David smirked. He studied Tanisha's face for her response.

"Whatever. It doesn't matter anyway, because I'm going with someone at my school," Tanisha blurted. She stared intently at the elevator buttons.

David turned Tanisha to face him. "You have a boyfriend, Tanisha? Why didn't you tell me that you had a boyfriend? You let me talk to you all night and never mentioned that you were going with someone."

"You didn't ask," Tanisha shrugged again, her expression stiff.

David dropped his hand from her shoulder and stared at her.

"But wait a minute. I thought you said that you can't date?" David asked.

The elevator was now on the third floor. "He's in eighth grade, and so I see him at school and on Fridays at the roller rink. He doesn't pick me up for dates," Tanisha offered dryly. Her voice was edgy.

"But you told me all about your family. I mean you could have mentioned that you're going with someone," David said.

"It's not that serious. Why does it matter anyway? Would you have not forced me to go for a walk with you and insisted on giving me a ski lesson if I'd told you that I was going with somebody?" Tanisha asked with irritation.

The elevator door opened and they stepped into the hallway. "No. It's cool. It's just that you didn't mention it that's all. What's his name?" Tanisha stopped at the door to her room.

"What's whose name?" Tanisha asked.

"What's your boyfriend's name?" David repeated. He studied Tanisha's face.

"His name is Darrell Hunter," Tanisha stammered. She swallowed hard.

"Listen. I'm gonna head back. I'll meet you at the ski rental place at ten o'clock," David said.

"You really don't have to give me a lesson, David," Tanisha said.

"I don't mind. You've never skied before, and you need a lesson. I said I would teach you how to ski, so I'll meet you at ten o'clock. Get some sleep, dress warmly and I'll see you in the morning." David watched Tanisha insert her key. He could hear her roommates chattering as Tanisha entered the room.

He walked down the hallway and pushed the elevator button. The elevator was still there. David pressed lobby and rode the slow elevator down. He paced back and forth. He was pissed. He had really enjoyed hanging out with Tanisha. So much so, that he was planning to go to Byron and tell him to back off. David was an upper classmen and Byron would back off if he told him to. But now Tanisha had told him that she was going with someone.

David knew what it meant to go with someone in eighth grade. The boy carried your backpack and chose you first for square dancing in P.E. class and you did the Fox Trot together at the roller skating rink on Friday nights. Occasionally, you were able to go to a movie together when you went with your group of friends and your girlfriend went with hers. The parents innocently dropped off the group of boys and girls and the couples paired up in the movie theatre. David had done this many times.

He also knew that eighth grade relationships were fragile and temporary and break ups happened weekly or sometimes daily. It was all part of the middle school mating game. The reasons were always silly. If your girlfriend's friend caught you smiling at another girl, expect a break up note. A different girlfriend saw you holding a door open for your girlfriend's arch enemy? Expect a break up note. You were seen getting another girl's number at the mall? Expect public humiliation. In public humiliation, your girlfriend would wait until all of your friends were around and break up with you as loudly as possible. All in an effort to reclaim her lost dignity. David had experienced several break-up notes and three public humiliation break ups since he'd started liking girls in eighth grade. He'd survived them all.

David knew that this Darrell Hunter guy was no match for him. He rubbed his hands together as the elevator crept slowly down the shaft. David was sixteen and drove a Corvette. He was clearly the most popular boy in his high school and could have any girl that he wanted. He stopped pacing and stared at the elevator buttons. Why was he sweating a fourteen year old eighth grader from Battle Creek Junior High School that he'd only known for over an hour?

"Hey, girls!" Tanisha said. She fastened the security lock on the door and walked into the room. Tanisha slipped off her shoes. Leslie and Vicky were in their pajamas. Each girl was lying across one of the double beds on her stomach facing the other. An *I Love Lucy* rerun was on the television. Both girls sat up on the bed. "I have to use the bathroom," Tanisha said.

"Girl, you better hurry up! I saw you leave with that fine ass David Barton. Where did you go and what did you do? We want details." Vicky's voice trailed as Tanisha slipped into the bathroom.

Tanisha closed the bathroom door and leaned against it. *Why did you lie to David about Darrell Hunter being your boyfriend?* She stared at her reflection in the mirror. She smacked her cheeks softly with her hand. *You are such a little liar. How are you going to keep all of these lies straight? Just because you were embarrassed that Byron flaunted his girlfriend in your face you told another lie! You're a liar! Liar, Liar pants on fire!*

"Tanisha! Hurry up in there, please! I have to use the bathroom," Leslie yelled from the bedroom.

Tanisha flushed the toilet and turned on the faucet. She splashed cold water on her face and stared at her reflection, as water dripped on her new sweater. *I'm even lying about using the bathroom! What's wrong with me?*

Chapter 13

The Crimson Tide

"Okay, Tanisha, I'm confused," Lori admitted. "So did you kick it with David Barton or not?"

"Well," Tanisha sighed. "He met me the next morning and gave me a ski lesson, but he wasn't as playful as he had been the night before. He was nice, but I could tell that he was only helping me because he'd said that he would," Tanisha said.

"Did you see Byron again?" Lori asked. She cupped her hand over the phone to yell at her sister who hovered over her shoulder. "Charlotte! Back off. I'll get off the phone when I'm good and ready. And the longer you listen to my conversation, the longer I'm going to stay on the phone so beat it! I'm sorry Tanisha, go ahead," Lori sighed.

"I saw Byron briefly," she continued. "He and his friends rode snow mobiles, but they didn't wear hats so he and his friend Tom got frost bite on their ears. I saw him that morning when they rented the snow mobiles. He spoke to me, but that was it. From what I heard, the frost bite was pretty bad so they had to go home on Saturday so they could see the doctor. The chaperones were planning to call their parents to pick them up, but David Barton agreed to drive them home so he left early too." Tanisha spoke quickly. She could hear Charlotte whining in the background.

"Did you see Maria or Rebecca again?' Lori asked.

"I sure did!" Tanisha said quickly. "Wait until you hear this one. I'll be quick because I know Charlotte is breathing down your neck. We didn't do anything Saturday night. The chaperones found out about the party at David Barton's on Friday, so they cancelled the teen mixer that was scheduled for Saturday and gave everybody a nine o'clock curfew. We were in bed by nine thirty. It was so boring. On Sunday morning, Leslie and Vicky wanted to sleep in so I went to brunch with two girls that I'd met skiing. As soon as we walked in, I saw Maria having brunch with Rebecca. They were eating and chatting like old pals! When I walked in, Maria whispered something to Rebecca and then Rebecca glared at me," she continued. "I know Maria told her that I liked Byron because after they finished eating Rebecca walked over to me and told me that I'd better stay away from her man. She pointed her finger in my face, so I grabbed her finger and held it for a second. I didn't say anything to her; I just held her finger and squeezed it tight. Maria didn't say a word. She just looked at me and left the restaurant with Rebecca," Tanisha finished.

"Okay, Charlotte, I'm getting off the phone now!" Lori groaned. "I don't know how Maria is going to act at school tomorrow. By the way, did Byron or David ask for your phone number?" Lori asked quickly.

"I don't know how Miss Maria is going to play that off tomorrow either. And nope! I didn't give out the digits. I don't think David liked me enough to ask for my number, especially when I told him that I had a boyfriend. He was funny and cool, but he's not really my type. You know I don't really like those cute, pretty boy types. And Byron isn't all that anyway," Tanisha groaned.

"You need to get over that pretty boy thing. Girl, if he likes you and you like him, go for it! Besides, I thought you said that David was nice," Lori reminded.

"He was nice. I mean, he is nice. He didn't ask for my phone number so it doesn't matter now. You better let me go so Charlotte can use the phone. I need to call Darrell anyway."

"Okay. I'll see you at lunch tomorrow," Lori said.

Tanisha hung up the phone and decided to work on her term paper. She read her title aloud. "Shakespeare, The World's Most Gifted Author: Fact or Fiction?" she groaned. "How the heck would I know? I haven't read all of the authors in the world," she continued. "Frankly, when it comes to reading stuff by dead guys, I prefer to read John Steinbeck or F. Scott Fitzgerald, but what do I know," she giggled. The outline complete, she needed to start writing the paper, but thinking of her English class assignment made her think about Maria.

She couldn't believe that they still weren't speaking. This was Tanisha's first experience with a friendship rift. In elementary school, she wasn't close to any of the white girls so she had no experience with a friend who wouldn't talk to her. Back then, none of her classmates talked to her unless they needed help with their school work and the teacher was busy. Tanisha always gladly helped them, hoping that they would befriend her, but it never worked. They continued to ignore her on the playground and at lunch. She had nicknamed herself the invisible brain.

Although she still had Lori and Rashanda and had grown closer to Justine and Grace, Tanisha missed Maria's friendship. She scribbled her initials in her notebook, doodled a picture of a flower and bit her pencil. She giggled and started writing.

Thesis: Black girls eat, white girls don't. Tanisha laughed out loud. *I wish Ms. Talaski had a sense of humor. I'd write a term paper on that.* She outlined a few key points.

1. Black girls eat macaroni and cheese as a side dish with dinner. White girls who eat macaroni and cheese eat it as an entrée and only eat as many noodles as they are old.

2. White girls drink diet soda. Black girls add sugar to regular soda.

3. Black girls sample from the food groups at every meal. White girls treat caffeine as a food group.

4. White girls eat lettuce. Black girls are allergic to lettuce.

Tanisha laughed heartily. *Can you be allergic to lettuce?* She'd observed the white girls at school picking at their lunch and gulping diet soda. *With her yo-yo dieting, and her desire to be ultra thin, Maria is acting like a white girl. And there's nothing I can do about it.* She tapped her pencil on her notebook. She tore up her silly thesis and outline and tossed it in the waste basket. *Even if I wanted to change my thesis, I don't have time to re-work this assignment. Get back to work, girlfriend!* She picked up her Shakespeare index cards and reviewed her notes.

Her teacher expected a fifteen page paper plus footnotes and a bibliography. Tanisha had never written a term paper and was intimidated by the assignment but was prepared to give it her best. English was one of her favorite subjects, and she was enjoying her research on William Shakespeare.

She had talked on the phone with Lori for well over an hour, spending most of her phone time lying across her bed upside down with her neck hanging over the edge. She lifted her body slowly to rebalance her equilibrium and decided that she'd get a snack before tackling more of her homework and calling Darrell. Plus, she still had to make those pork chops for dinner.

On her way to the kitchen she stopped to use the bathroom. When she pulled down her panties to pee, she was shocked to see a stain in the center of her panties. The stain was thick and dark brown. Confused, she stared at the stain intently. She thought that it might be her period, but the stain didn't look like blood. She wiped between her legs and studied the tissue. The stain on the tissue was bright red. It was blood. Tanisha's period had started.

In the books that she'd read about what her first period would be like, she'd expected her stomach to cramp and the blood flow to resemble the trickle of urine. But her period had started while she lay on the bed chatting on the phone with Lori. Tanisha hadn't felt a thing.

She looked under the sink for one of Billie's sanitary napkins but instead found a blue box with pink writing. The word TAMPONS was spelled out in large block letters. *Tampons?* None of the literature that Tanisha had read mentioned tampons. Tanisha picked up the box and read the directions and confirmed that the tampons were used for menstrual flow. She didn't know how to use a tampon. Of her friends, Lori and Maria were the only two who had gotten their period. Tanisha clearly *couldn't* call Maria, so she had to call Lori. Tanisha stuffed tissue in between her legs and raced back to her room. She pulled the pink princess phone as far as she could and was grateful when the cord reached into the bathroom. She dialed Lori's house. Charlotte answered the phone on the first ring.

"Hey, Charlotte. This is Tanisha. May I speak to Lori, please?"

"I'm on the phone, Tanisha," Charlotte said gruffly.

"Charlotte, I know you're not on the phone yet, you're waiting for a call. Come on, it's an emergency and will only take one minute I promise," Tanisha pleaded.

Charlotte liked Tanisha and agreed to give Lori the phone under the condition that the phone call would only last one minute.

"Hey, girl, what's up?" Lori chewed as she spoke.

"I think I just got my period!" Tanisha squealed.

"Congratulations! Welcome to the club!"

"Do you know how to use a tampon?" Tanisha asked.

"I don't use them, but Charlotte does. Just use a sanitary napkin," Lori suggested.

"I can't find any so let me talk to Charlotte real quick." Tanisha wiped herself again and saw bright red blood on the tissue this time.

Charlotte gave Tanisha a ten second instruction on tampon insertion and quickly hung up the phone. She was less than helpful. Tanisha found a small instruction sheet in the box of tampons and read. She pried off the wrapper and studied the cardboard tampon. The tampon was about four inches long. She was confused by the instruction to insert with one hand and pull the cardboard with the other hand. She also didn't know where to insert the tampon. She'd never studied her private parts closely before and didn't realize that the tampon did not get inserted in the area where the urine flow occurred. As she attempted to insert the tampon in the urine tract, she moaned in pain. *Aha! Now I understand the pain that I read about when your period starts.* As she struggled with the tampon, she heard Billie Mae moving around in her bedroom.

Tanisha stared at her reflection in the mirror. She was scared to face Billie, but she needed help. She didn't know what to do. *Please, God. Let Billie, I mean mom, be in a good mood!* She tossed the tampon in the trash, stuffed a wad of toilet tissue in her panties to catch the blood, washed her hands and walked cautiously into Billie Mae's room.

"Hey, Mom," she said nervously. "I think I just got my period. Do you have any sanitary napkins?" Tanisha asked quickly before Billie turned around to greet her. She could feel her heart beating a mile a minute.

Billie Mae stared at her for a few seconds without responding. "No. I'm out. Your period started?" Her voice still had a sleepy tone.

"Yes. I think it just started a few minutes ago. I saw blood in my underwear," she said softly.

"Give me a few minutes, and I'll take you to the store to get some," Billie offered.

"Okay. I was having trouble with my homework so I haven't cooked dinner yet, but I'll cook when we get back," Tanisha lied. She didn't want her mother to know that she had been on the phone with Lori for well over an hour.

"Don't worry about it. I'll cook when we get back." Billie smoothed the comforter on her bed. Tanisha raced to her room to get her wallet. They drove in silence for the five minute ride to the neighborhood drugstore. Billie maneuvered the car parallel to the curb in the grocery pick up lane and lit a cigarette. "I'll wait here for you," she said. "Here's ten dollars. I usually buy Kotex but buy whatever kind you like. That should be enough. And pick up a gallon of milk, too."

Tanisha took the ten dollar bill, jumped out of the car and went inside to purchase her first feminine hygiene product. She walked carefully so that the wad of tissue nestled between her legs didn't slip out of her panties. As she searched for the sanitary napkin aisle, Tanisha stopped dead in her tracks and tried to remember the last time that Billie had given her money.

She's being awfully nice. It's hard to believe that this is the same woman that almost bit my head off an hour ago. Maybe Billie took some of the medication that her boss Kaye mentioned before her nap. Does mental medication work that quickly?

Chapter 14

A Case of Mistaken Identity

Maria and Rashanda had started spending a lot of time together. Rashanda knew that she was caught in the middle of a teenage drama triangle between Tanisha, Lori and Maria. Monday night, she'd heard an abbreviated version of Tanisha's John & Judy ski trip story from Lori. Since the rift over her Todd inspired weight loss plan, Maria had socially isolated herself from Lori and Tanisha, or as much as she could, considering the number of classes that she and Tanisha shared. She continued to eat lunch at their table every day but barely spoke to either of them.

In Humanities class, Maria had requested to have her seat switched so that she was not sitting with the other girls. Rashanda was torn. She liked Maria and enjoyed having Maria all to herself for a change, but she also enjoyed spending time with Lori and Tanisha. She was glad that Maria hadn't asked her to choose between her friendship and Lori and Tanisha's. Rashanda just wished that things could go back to being the way they were.

The girls continued to go to the skating rink every Friday, but since Tanisha and Lori had confronted Maria about her thinness, Maria only carpooled with the other girls if Rashanda's mom drove the carpool. Once there, Maria would disappear with Todd until it was time to be picked up.

"Rashanda, why don't you see if your parents will let you get contacts?" Maria asked.

"I've asked, but they won't let me get contacts until next year." Rashanda picked at a piece of meat stuck in her braces.

"Oh, that's too bad. Todd has a friend that he's bringing to the skating rink on Friday, and I wanted to introduce you to him. I think you look better without your glasses," Maria coached.

"I agree, but I can't see very well without my glasses. I can see a little bit but things are blurry and fuzzy. But I could bring my eyeglass case and take them off once we got inside the skating rink," Rashanda offered.

"Good idea! His friend's name is David, and Todd asked me to introduce him to one of my friends at the rink on Friday."

The friend that Todd referred to was David Barton. David and Todd's parents were friends and the two boys had practically grown up together. When Todd mentioned to David that his latest "middle school conquest" was a girl named Maria who attended Battle Creek Junior High School, David remembered that Tanisha had mentioned a classmate named Maria who lived near a tennis court, and suspected that it might be Todd's Maria.

David desperately wanted to see Tanisha again. When he helped her with her ski lesson on Saturday morning, Tanisha was playful and comical, but David was quiet. He helped her pick out the proper skis for her height and weight, and showed her how to snap her ski boots into her ski binders. This required him to briefly place his arms around her waist. The brief physical closeness to Tanisha excited him.

He held her hand and guided her to the bunny slope and showed her how to bend her knees and lean into her ski boots to plow down the hill. Initially, Tanisha's stance was awkward and clumsy and she fell several times. David skied over to her and showed her how to use her ski poles to pull herself back up. Once, Tanisha playfully pulled David into the snow with her, and David laughed briefly and then his serious distracted look returned. When Tanisha gazed at David with a puzzled expression and asked him what was wrong, David responded that he was still pissed with his friend that had thrown up in his room the night before, complaining that the stench had lingered all night. This was a cover up story. The housekeeping staff had thoroughly cleaned up the mess and David's room was sparkling clean with no odor at all.

Tanisha could sense that David was clearly distracted and thought that he was bored with her slow skiing progress. She decided to spare him anymore teaching torture and ended the ski lesson early, telling David that she was ready to call it quits and take a break. She declined his offer to buy her a hot chocolate.

David had agreed to drive Byron and Tom home early from the ski resort in an effort to avoid seeing Tanisha again on Saturday. David really liked her and was afraid that if he spent any more time with her he would pour out his feelings and share how hurt he'd been when she told him that she had a boyfriend. He couldn't believe that he was feeling that strongly about a fourteen year old girl. He was almost seventeen and had been dating for over two years. He had never felt the way he was feeling about any of the girls that he'd dated in the past.

David had been thinking about Tanisha every day since the ski trip and thought about asking Leslie for her number. But then he reconsidered. He was a junior in high school. How could he ask Leslie for an eighth grader's phone number? He couldn't think of a plausible story to explain why he wanted her number. No, he couldn't involve Leslie, so he was relieved when Todd mentioned Maria at golf the following week.

"I thought I saw you walking around with a new one on your arm in Lake Geneva. Was that Maria?" David asked.

"That was her. She's cute, but I think she's getting a little pudgy. I told her that I like my girls lean and mean," Todd boasted.

"Pudgy? She looks like she barely weighs one hundred pounds. You're tripping, Todd," David said, his face scrunched into a scowl.

"I don't want her to lose weight. I just think she needs to lift weights and develop some muscle tone and lose that baby fat. I'm an athlete, and I like my girls toned and buffed." Todd flexed his bicep.

"Excuse me, Mr. Universe! By the way, how's Felicia? Does she know about your middle school honey?" David asked.

Felicia was a sophomore in high school and had been dating Todd off and on since freshman year.

"Naw. Felicia has no idea. She thinks that I go to the skating rink every Friday to watch my little sister skate. My parents are so happy that I take her and pick her up," Todd chuckled. "But it's the only way I can hook up with Maria unless she's at a friend's house, and I pick her up from over there and we disappear for a few hours. But usually, she goes to the skating rink with her friends on Friday nights, and we do our thing in my car. Felicia doesn't like to skate, and she thinks it's cute that I bond with my little sister. She's so clueless," he laughed.

David didn't understand why Todd felt the need to cheat on Felicia but he knew that he'd been seeing other girls for awhile. Most of the girls that Todd dated on the side were eighth graders. David had scolded Todd about dating girls that were so young, so he was too embarrassed to share with Todd that he'd met Tanisha who was only fourteen and a classmate of Maria's. He didn't want to feel like a hypocrite.

"Well, maybe I'll go with you to the rink this Friday. I haven't skated in a while and I could use the exercise," David suggested.

"Now you're talking! Welcome to my world! These middle school girls are hot! Some of them don't even look like they're in junior high school. Maria always comes with a crew of girls so I'll introduce you to some of her friends," he boasted. "A couple of her friends are still going through that middle school, pudgy awkward stage," he laughed. "But her friend Tanisha is kinda cute," he paused. "And there's this tall girl with long, reddish blonde hair who has a lot of potential, but she has bad posture and acts mousy," Todd finished.

"Bingo!" David said loudly grinning from ear to ear.

"What did you say?" Todd asked.

David shook his head from side to side. "I said what does mousy mean?"

Todd burped loudly. "She acts like she's afraid of her own shadow," he explained. "Like she's a timid little mouse," he laughed. "But I like my girls timid and tame so I can bring out the wildcat in them! That's why I fish in the middle school pond," he shared. "But you have to be careful, because these middle school girls are quick to fall in love with the first boy who gives them the time of day. They haven't developed the veteran slickness of the high school girls yet," he laughed.

"You are such a pig! You have a sick, twisted mind, Todd," David scolded. "And slow down there, Sporty. I'm not trolling the middle school girls like you, but if you're huddled up with Maria all night, at least I'll have someone to talk to," David smiled. "And I could use the exercise," he added quickly.

"You can say that again. Your six pack is turning into a keg, tubby," Todd teased patting David's rock hard abdomen.

David punched Todd in the stomach. Todd responded by tackling David to the ground. David effortlessly flipped over sitting on his friend and pinning him down by his shoulders.

"I'm not going to let you up until you admit that you're a fat little, pig," David laughed. "Say it!" he ordered.

"Okay," Todd stammered. "I'm a fat little pig. Oink Oink!"

Chapter 15

Turnabout

The Chicago area weather was very unpredictable. Two weeks earlier, a winter storm watch was in effect and snow blanketed the ground. Now, the temperature hovered in the low fifties and the tree buds were blooming. Tanisha enjoyed the chirping birds that sang outside of her bedroom window. That morning she'd seen a small dead bird on the front porch. She looked up and saw twigs peeking out of the gutter above her bedroom window. A bird had nested on their roof.

Nesting birds and blooming trees brought with them the promise of warmer weather and the spring dance. The halls of Battle Creek Junior High were abuzz about the Turnabout dance. Tanisha and Darrell had agreed to carpool to the dance with CJ and Lori. In the time honored Sadie Hawkins tradition, the girls were responsible for every detail of the date including the transportation arrangements. Lori's mom had agreed to pick them up after the dance was over and take everyone home. Tanisha was responsible for coordinating the pick-ups to the dance. Fortunately, CJ's parents were dropping him off at Lori's house for pictures and Lori only lived three blocks away from Darrell, so there would only be two stops involved.

She'd asked Jack first, but he was scheduled to work at the bank Friday night. He had offered to switch with someone if Billie couldn't take them. Tanisha hated to make her brother change his work schedule so she squared her shoulders and counted to ten.

Tanisha was nervous that Billie would refuse, since she knew that Billie normally went to a Buddhist meeting every Friday night, but she knew that she had to ask. She had no choice. Her dad worked nights, plus, it wasn't practical for him to drive in from the city to take them. And truthfully, Tanisha didn't want her dad to meet Darrell. Her dad knew that she was going to the dance, but she'd downplayed the fact that she was going with a boy, and had told him that she was going with a group of friends. As she prepared to ask Billie, she took a deep breath and knocked on her bedroom door. Billie was busy folding a stack of clothes that had become a permanent fixture on the floor in the corner of her room.

"Mom?" Tanisha slowly exhaled the air in her lungs, cleared her throat and continued talking rapidly. "Sorry to bother you, but the Turnabout Dance is this Friday, and I've asked Darrell Hunter to go. You remember him. He's in the student council with me. Anyway, since the girl asks the boy, I'm supposed to pick him up. Lori's mother can bring us home, so I was wondering if you could pick up Darrell and Lori and CJ. CJ is going to be at Lori's house already, so you only have to make two stops." Tanisha paused and held her breath in anticipation. She braced herself for the quick no.

"Sure. No problem. What time is the dance?" Billie continued to fold the clothes and lay them neatly across her bed.

"It starts at seven o'clock, so we can leave at six thirty." Tanisha exhaled and her eyes widened to the size of saucers as she spoke. She was shocked that she hadn't had to beg and plead for a ride. Her eyes continued to study the room. Billie's dresser was neat and her closet had been reorganized. She noticed an empty space where Billie's Buddhist altar had been. She'd moved it from the living room to her bedroom so that she could chant without disturbing Allen and Byron as they watched the only color television in the house. Tanisha's eyes spanned the room looking for the altar. Two large black trash bags were propped against the closet door. Sweaters were folded neatly on the closet shelf and her shoes were neatly lined below.

"Okay. What time is the dance over?" Billie asked.

"The dance ends at nine o'clock, but we are going to grab a bite to eat at Sanfratello's Pizza in River. Mrs. Perkins is picking us up from there," Tanisha explained.

"How are you going to get to Sanfratello's?" Billie brushed by Tanisha to place some clothes in her drawer. "Excuse me for bumping into you."

"That's okay," Tanisha replied stunned. "We were going to walk. It's only five blocks," Tanisha responded. She was blown away by Billie's politeness. A few days ago Billie had bumped into her and yelled "Move!" Her tone was so loud that Tanisha almost cried.

"I don't want you to walk at night. It's dangerous. I'll pick you up at the dance at nine o'clock and take you to Sanfratello's and Mrs. Perkins can pick you up from there. Are the girls paying for the pizza?" Billie walked back over to the bed and picked up another stack of neatly folded clothes.

"Uh, huh. We're supposed to pay for everything since it's the Sadie Hawkins dance," Tanisha explained.

"Do you need any money?" Billie asked.

*Tanisha couldn't believe what she was hearing. Billie was offering to **give** her money?*

"No. I think I have enough. Lori and I are splitting the pizza expense. But thanks for asking," Tanisha replied.

"By the way, your father is buying you a new bed and a dresser. He's going to take you to Sears this weekend to pick it out. You're too big for that little twin size bed," Billie stated. "I went in your room today, and I think your old mattress still smells like urine from when you wet the bed when you were little," she finished.

When I was little? Tanisha had wet the bed almost nightly. She was wearing an adult size five shoe, and still wet the bed. She wasn't little. By fourth grade her bed wetting accidents occurred less frequently. And by fifth grade she was not wetting the bed at all, often awakening in the middle of the night to use the bathroom.

Tanisha believed that her parents were so caught up in their own drama that they hadn't noticed that she was still wetting the bed. She'd been taught to do her own laundry when she was seven years old and her parents seldom entered her room. The only lingering reminder of her bed wetting ordeal was the gaping hole in her twin mattress, the smell of dried urine, and the scrapes that she got on her legs from the rusted springs in her mattress.

"Okay." Tanisha didn't know what else to say. Billie had changed. Tanisha had noticed different behavior from her mom after the John & Judy ski trip, but she hadn't overheard any conversations to understand what had driven the change. Whatever the cause, Tanisha was just glad that she wasn't treading around Billie like broken glass.

"I hope it doesn't make you late for your Buddhist meeting," Tanisha tested. Her eyes still wandered the room looking for signs of the Buddhist altar.

"I've stopped practicing Buddhism. How was your day?" Billie asked.

"Oh. It was fine. I'd better go start my homework." Tanisha walked out of the room with her eyebrow raised. *She offered to give me money, she's being nice, the Buddhist altar is gone, and now Billie has arranged for me to get a new bed? What's going on with her?*

Chapter 16

In the Beginning

Slowly fingering the brown prescription bottle in her hand, she sighed loudly, shaking her head at her new world. She quickly tucked the bottle back into its hiding place. She'd been told that she would have to take medication for the rest of her life. Her mental health depended on it.

She stared at a brown angora sweater that she'd bought her senior year in high school. She studied the sweater carefully. Surprised that the sweater hadn't been eaten by moths after all these years, she casually tossed it into the goodwill pile before changing her mind, folding it and placing it on the "keep" pile. "Tanisha might want that sweater. It was expensive, and it's a classic," she said aloud. Cleaning had suddenly become therapeutic for Billie. She continued organizing her room and rearranging the clothes in her closet which provided an unexpected walk down memory lane. Her parents had purchased that sweater for her to make her feel better.

Since she was about eleven years old, Billie had suspected that something was wrong with her, but she struggled to describe the way she was feeling in a way that made sense to anyone else. "I just don't like myself," she'd say to her parents when they questioned her about her mood swings. "It feels like someone else is controlling my thoughts half the time," she'd plead. But they would just stare at her with puzzled expressions, sigh and give her money to buy herself something before walking away.

As she grew older, she continued to fight regularly with her parents and ran away from home several times. Her behavior was explained by the police as typical teenage rebellion. Each time she came home, she was punished and her privileges were restricted. At first, her parents blamed themselves. But later, they shifted the blame to her privileged upbringing and labeled her spoiled, boy crazy and unappreciative.

But Billie knew deep down inside that something else was going on with her. For years, she'd felt that something was wrong with her mind, but she didn't know how to ask for help. She didn't understand the conflict waging war inside her head. To her, it felt like a battle between good and evil. On good days she spoke rapidly, laughing easily and rushing to finish her household chores and school projects. On bad days, she scowled at everyone and harbored hateful thoughts toward her parents, siblings, teachers, friends and even herself. At first, everyone thought it was severe PMS, but the bad days lasted longer than the three or four days of her menstrual cycle. Once again she was labeled. This time her label was moody and mean. Her siblings ignored her and her friends grew to distrust her and stayed away. When her bad day sequence morphed into a good day, and she tried to reconnect with people, no one wanted anything to do with her. It was a lonely existence. She started keeping a journal to write down her feelings.

Billie pulled the journal from a box of memorabilia that her parents had sent her when they cleaned out their attic. She rubbed the cover of the leather bound journal and squeezed it to her chest. She went to the bookmark and opened the journal to the date of her last entry. *December 31, 1963.* She smiled to herself. That was the night that Jack was conceived. She read the three line entry that she'd written that morning.

Dear Diary,

Tonight is the night. I hope "the party" is all that I'd planned. I hope there are Fireworks and sparks. bmp

The thick journal was mostly empty, so even if her parents had read it, they wouldn't have read anything juicy. Besides, most of her journal entries were written in code to safeguard her privacy. She sighed again. She only wrote in the journal when she was feeling happy, which wasn't that often.

She was surprised that she hadn't written in the journal a few days after her first dalliance with Jackie Carlson since she had enjoyed "the party" a great deal. And then she remembered that her journal had come up missing until her parents found it in their attic a few years ago. Billie suspected that her sister Shanay had stolen her journal to read it in the attic and left it up there. Billie was so consumed with her pregnancy and her quick wedding to Jackie that she'd forgotten about the journal. Although Billie enjoyed being pregnant, especially the attention she received as a pregnant lady, she hadn't bothered to journal during her pregnancy. And after she delivered Jack, she'd been severely depressed. Once again, she found herself labeled, this time with post partum depression.

Her post partum depression was more severe than the baby blues that some new moms experience as a result of shifting hormonal levels after childbirth. Billie Mae's episodes were labeled psychoses after childbirth and required hospitalization and medication. If she'd found the journal during this time, she would have burned it. She clutched the journal to her chest and thought about her life as a young mother.

After Jack was born, Billie was transferred from the maternity ward to the psychiatric ward. When the nurses tried to get her to hold her newborn son, she refused and screamed until they sedated her with medication. After several attempts to get her to interact with her baby, the doctors recommended to Jackie that he have her committed for psychiatric observation. During that time, Jackie's sister Bethany and her husband cared for Jack while Jackie worked. Eight months later, Billie came home and tried to learn how to mother her new infant under the close and watchful eye of Jackie's mother, Grandma Bootsy. Billie was barely out of the psychiatric hospital when she became pregnant with Tanisha. After Tanisha was born, Billie's thoughts became so severely psychotic that she was afraid of Tanisha. When she looked at Tanisha, she imagined that Tanisha was a wild chicken poised to attack her. Billie feared that she would strangle Tanisha, and refused to touch her. Once again, she was transferred from the maternity ward to the psychiatric ward.

When they were first married, Jackie and Billie lived upstairs in a building owned by Grandma Bootsy. During Billie's hospitalization after Tanisha's birth, Grandma Bootsy fed, bathed, nurtured and loved Tanisha and Jack while Jackie worked. This time Billie was hospitalized for four months. Billie remembered Jackie bringing her brown angora sweater and tan corduroy pants to the hospital the day before she was discharged.

Pink, yellow, red and green balloons floated in the air. A welcome home banner was draped across the living room wall. She remembered that all of Jackie's siblings were there, and they each hugged her when she walked in the apartment. She hugged Jack and smiled as Grandma Bootsy walked toward her with a baby in her arms. Billie had been secretly dreading this moment. It was Billie's daughter, Tanisha, whom she'd not held or touched in four months.

Grandma Bootsy carefully placed Tanisha in Billie's arms. Billie raised the tiny baby up to her face and stared into her eyes. She hadn't really looked at her baby in the hospital. Her daughter looked like Jackie's sister Helen. Billie rolled her eyes. She hated

Helen. She inhaled Tanisha's scent and frowned slightly, careful to avoid detection from the closely watching family members.

Billie handed Tanisha back to Grandma Bootsy and politely asked her to give the baby a bath. Grandma Bootsy glanced at Jackie who just shrugged. She had just bathed Tanisha, but bathed her again to satisfy Billie's request. This time, Billie supervised the bath, handing her mother-in-law the baby products herself. Grandma Bootsy dried Tanisha and dressed her in fresh clothes. She handed Tanisha to Billie again. Billie inhaled deeply. This time she gagged as though she would vomit. She returned Tanisha to Grandma Bootsy and announced that she wasn't feeling well. She left her welcome home party and walked upstairs to her bedroom to take a nap.

As Billie lay across the bed, she realized that she still harbored psychotic thoughts of harming Tanisha. When she looked at her daughter she thought she looked like a chicken, and she wanted to ring her neck. She hated herself for thinking that she wanted to harm her own flesh and blood.

Billie remembered Jack toddling into the bedroom and laying beside her. She remembered gently placing her arm across her son's shoulders and embracing him. She smelled his head. He smelled fine. And then it hit her. Billie just didn't like the way that Tanisha smelled. She couldn't explain it, but Jack's smell was different and (for whatever reason) tolerable to Billie.

Jackie had met with Billie's psychiatrists and knew that many women suffer mild depression after childbirth due to the changing hormonal levels. The doctors explained that sometimes it takes months for mothers to form a maternal bond with their infants, especially when the infant and mother have been separated for extended periods of time as was the case with Billie and Tanisha. So Jackie and Grandma Bootsy cared for Tanisha. Fearing for the baby's safety, they agreed never to leave Billie alone with her daughter.

Billie and Jackie still lived upstairs in the small apartment owned by Grandma Bootsy, and Tanisha spent most of her time toddling up and down the stairs to snuggle next to her beloved grandmother and play with Grandma Bootsy's dog, Duke, a German Shepherd Labrador mix who ate corn flakes with milk for breakfast and allowed Tanisha to kiss him on the snout. Sometimes, Tanisha napped on the floor with Duke snuggled by her side.

Byron was born almost two years after Tanisha. After his birth, the Carlson family braced itself for Billie Mae to have another psychotic episode, but she surprised everyone and did not require hospitalization. Billie breastfed Byron and nurtured him like he was her first born. Jackie was grateful that his mom was retired and lived in the apartment just below which allowed her to keep a sharp eye out for her grandchildren while Jackie went to work. But the tiny two bedroom apartment was now much too small for a growing family, so Jackie was forced to look for a bigger place. Shortly after Byron's birth, the family moved across town into a small bungalow on Chicago's south side. Grandma Bootsy came over every day to help Billie with the children. Billie now forced herself to change her daughter's diaper or feed her, but she was still repulsed by Tanisha's scent. She was afraid to share this with anyone for fear that they would send her back to the mental hospital.

Although Jackie and Billie agreed that it would be best for her mental health not to have any more children, Billie had been raised in Catholic schools and believed that taking birth control pills was a sin. She was too embarrassed to go to the pharmacist to have the prescription filled for the contraceptive pill. She soon became pregnant with Allen. Immediately after Allen was born, Billie had a severe psychotic episode. Days after delivering Allen and being released from the hospital, with Jack in tow, she ran out of the house screaming that someone was trying to kill her. Jackie feared that Billie would harm one of the children and called the police for assistance to subdue her. He had her committed to the mental health ward for observation. She was hospitalized for five months. Grandma Bootsy moved in with the family while Billie was hospitalized. Tanisha was only five years old but Billie still remembered what Tanisha said to her the day that she came home from the psychiatric hospital.

"I hate you, Mommy! I don't want you here! Why don't you go back to the hospital so Grandma Bootsy can stay with us? I wish you were dead!" Tanisha screamed at Billie before attempting to kick her in the knee.

Tanisha's words cut Billie to the core. Years later, the words still hung in the air like a dark cloud following her around. Whenever she looked at Tanisha, she was reminded of those words. Billie tried to recall what it was about Tanisha's scent as an infant that she found so distasteful, but she couldn't remember. There was nothing in her life now that triggered the foul scent that she associated with her own flesh and blood, an odor that had formed a wedge between her and her only daughter. Billie had been like a dog whose puppy had been handled by a human and carried their offensive scent. She'd rejected her own offspring like a bitch rejects its puppy.

As her children grew older, Billie struggled to manage her chemical imbalance but refused to take the prescribed medications consistently. She hadn't had an episode since Allen's birth and believed that she was better, but her mood swings and erratic behavior were unpredictable. As far as she knew, her children were unaware of her condition. And she was too ashamed to discuss it with them. She wore the stigma of her mental illness like an invisible cloak.

Billie had managed to form a relationship with her sons, but as Tanisha grew older, the distance between them had grown wider. Now, years later, Billie had to face the harsh reality that she had never formed a maternal bond with Tanisha. They were like strangers who shared a common genetic makeup.

She placed the journal back in its hiding place on her closet shelf and paused. She pulled the journal down, stared at it, and contemplated destroying such a visible reminder of her troubled past. She bit her lip and decided to keep the journal, tucking it snugly back into her closet.

Her road to better was now a couple of weeks old. She'd started by taking her medication and trying to improve her children's home life. Her fascination with Buddhism had faded. When her chanting didn't bring her the prosperity and wealth that she desired, she swore off the practice. She tossed out her altar and incense unceremoniously. Her Buddhist buddies called the house, but Billie refused to speak with them.

Her medication helped her to think clearly. It made her sleepy, but it helped control the raging thoughts in her head. She became less paranoid and was more receptive to feedback. She cooked meals for her children and tidied up the house. She also attended Byron's soccer games and spent her days searching the classified ads for employment opportunities.

Once her medication stabilized her mental state, Billie called her boss at Eden Prairie and met her for lunch. Billie confessed that she was bipolar and was now committed to taking her medication regularly. As sympathetic as Kaye was to Billie's condition, she could not arrange for Billie to return to the university. The department head had decided that the manner in which Billie had resigned without giving any notice made her ineligible to return to the university. But Kaye pledged to violate university policy and provide a good reference for Billie to help her get another job.

Billie was glad that she would be able to help Tanisha by taking her friends to the spring dance. Her doctor had told her to take baby steps and not expect everyone to warm up quickly to the new and improved Billie. She'd also cautioned her that the bipolar condition could be effectively managed but only if she committed to taking her medications for the rest of her life.

Billie took a deep breath and walked out of the closet. She was in this for the long haul.

Chapter 17

All Dressed Up and Nowhere to Go

On Turnabout Dance Friday, the girls met in the cafeteria for their daily lunch meeting. Maria had warmed slightly to Lori but was still frosty to Tanisha. Maria and Rashanda chatted about their plans to go to the skating rink that evening.

"My mom can take us if your mom can pick us up," Rashanda said.

"Okay. Or I could just tell my mom that your mom is dropping us off and picking us up. That way, Todd can give us a ride home, and he and I can spend more time together," Maria suggested. Rashanda was not comfortable with that idea. Like the other girls, Rashanda was not allowed to date and knew that her parents wouldn't approve of her riding in a car with a boy, unless it was Tanisha's brother Jack.

"I don't know about that, Maria. What if my mom wants to talk to your mom?" Rashanda asked.

"She won't. Trust me. It will be fine. We'll just have him drop us off a few doors down from our actual houses in case one of the parents is looking out of the window. Don't fake on me now, Rashanda. Todd's expecting me to bring some friends for his friend David Barton to talk to," Maria pleaded. She took a small bite from her apple.

Tanisha had been giggling with Lori about their Turnabout Dance plans, but her ears perked up when Maria mentioned the name David Barton.

"Besides, he told me that David has a Corvette and he may want to take you home himself," Maria winked. "I saw him on the ski trip, and he is cute! I'd try to snag him myself, but he's Todd's best friend," she laughed.

David? Corvette? Tanisha couldn't believe it. Rashanda was planning to meet David Barton at the skating rink tonight? Before Tanisha could digest what she'd just heard, Lori chimed in.

"Did you say David Barton?" Lori asked. She continued before Maria could respond. "Isn't that the guy that you met on that ski trip, Tanisha?"

Tanisha had planned to ignore Maria's comments but now she couldn't avoid responding. She chewed her pizza, swallowed and mumbled. "Uh huh, that's him."

"**You** know David Barton?" Maria's tone was caustic and condescending. "How did **you** meet him?" she asked sarcastically. Her eyes roamed up and down Tanisha's frame.

Tanisha glared at Maria with an icy expression. "I met him at his private party on Friday night in Lake Geneva, and then we went for a walk and talked. He also gave me a private ski lesson on Saturday morning before he left early to take Byron and Tom home for frostbite," she finished boldly.

Her face softer now, Maria raised an eyebrow, her mouth opened to speak, but no words were uttered. She just stared curiously at Tanisha.

Tanisha studied Rashanda across the table and smiled softly. She was too proper to say what she was thinking, but she knew that Rashanda was not David's type. Rashanda's under-construction appearance (two ponytails, braces and glasses) was just not sophisticated enough for a high school boy's taste. She wasn't getting any attention from the boys in junior high school yet. Besides, Tanisha had spent enough time with David to know that Rashanda lacked the wit to keep David amused. *Stop slicing her apart, Tanisha! She's your friend. Besides, you don't know what someone's type is. You clearly weren't his type. He didn't even ask for your phone number, Tanisha.*

"He's a nice guy, Rashanda," Tanisha said softly. "You'll have fun with him. In fact, tell him I said hello when you see him," she said, smiling warmly at her friend.

Lori studied Tanisha's face. She quickly pulled out her notebook and a pen and jotted a note to Tanisha. She discreetly slid the note across the table to her friend.

T, Aren't you pissed that Rashanda is meeting "your" David tonight?

The your in the note was underlined several times. Tanisha ripped the note into tiny pieces and stuffed it into her empty chocolate milk container. "He's not mine," Tanisha mouthed slowly. Lori stared at Tanisha curiously. Tanisha shrugged and finished her lunch seconds before the bell rang.

Billie was actually looking forward to driving Tanisha and her friends to the Turnabout Dance. Her day had gotten off to a good start. She'd had a job interview for an executive assistant role at the local cable company that morning which looked very promising. Billie was in a good mood.

She'd been taking her lithium pills daily and could feel a difference in her temperament. She decided to get the car washed and vacuumed so that Tanisha's friends could ride in a clean vehicle. She'd bought the car second hand, but it was only five years old, and she enjoyed the luxury that it offered with its soft charcoal gray leather seats and spacious interior. While vacuuming the car, she found a twenty dollar bill in the seat. Billie's day kept getting better and better.

She'd just had a civil conversation with her ex-husband, Jackie who had called to see if Billie could bring the children into the city on Saturday for Grandma Bootsy's birthday party.

Jackie was accustomed to driving from the city to Newberry East every weekend to spend time with his children and would often pick the children up for family events in Chicago and have to bring them home the same evening. His occasional requests for Billie to drop the kids off were always rejected by Billie. But today, Billie was polite and agreed to drop Tanisha, Byron and Allen at Bootsy's house Saturday evening to spare Jackie from making two trips into the city since Jack, Jr. had plans Saturday evening. Billie had turned over a new leaf!

Tanisha wasn't really looking forward to going to the Turnabout Dance with Darrell. He was the most popular boy in eighth grade and Tanisha had never been on a "date" before, but she wasn't as excited as she thought she would be. She scowled at her dress choice and suddenly felt self conscious about wearing a sleeveless summer sun dress in April. But it was too late now. It was the only dressy outfit that she had. She'd wanted to buy a new dress for the dance, but she decided that she'd rather spend her money on a new outfit to impress Byron, and after the ski outfits that she purchased, she didn't have enough money left to also buy a new dress. She looked at herself in the bathroom mirror and decided that she'd primped enough for Mr. Darrell Hunter. He'd called her almost every night to discuss the Turnabout Dance, but her infatuation with him had grown cold. Tanisha really didn't want to go but knew that it was too late to back out now.

Tanisha slipped on her white wedge sandals and went downstairs to leave for the dance.

"You look pretty, Tanisha. Do you want to wear some of my

make-up?" Billie asked.

Tanisha was still not completely comfortable with Billie's newfound niceness and looked at her with a sideways glance but decided that a little make-up might be in order for a school dance.

"Sure, why not?" Tanisha replied somberly.

Billie applied mascara to Tanisha's eyelashes and a little blush to her cheeks. She decided that Tanisha didn't need more than lip gloss to highlight her full lips. She also fluffed Tanisha's hair out and gave her a pink shawl that she'd knitted several years before so that Tanisha would have a cover for her shoulders. Tanisha thought the shawl looked old fashioned, but she knew she'd need something to ward off the late night April chill and she didn't have an appropriate spring jacket, so she agreed to carry it.

Billie and Tanisha picked up Lori and CJ first before picking up Darrell. When they pulled up in front of Darrell's house, Tanisha was glad that Billie decided to get out of the car to meet his parents. Billie looked pretty in black wool slacks and a red v-neck sweater as she met Mr. and Mrs. Hunter. Tanisha was shocked when Billie didn't correct Darrell when he introduced her to his parents as Mrs. Carlson. Darrell looked handsome in a black suit with a white shirt and yellow tie.

"You look nice, Tanisha." Darrell beamed a wide smile at Tanisha that showed his mouth full of metal braces. She squinted, noticing something stuck in his braces.

"Thanks, Darrell, so do you," Tanisha said softly.

Darrell handed Tanisha a wrist corsage that was tucked in a plastic box with a clear lid. Inside the box were two pink carnations held together by a light pink ribbon. *Pink? He knew that I was wearing yellow! We've talked about my dress for two weeks. Why would he buy pink carnations when he knew I was wearing yellow? What a moron!*

Tanisha was ready to end the date before it started. She

thought the pink wrist corsage was hideous. She painted a smile on her face and opened the container. Slipping the corsage on her wrist, she pursed her lips together and smiled sweetly. *Well, at least the ugly corsage matches my shawl.*

With the girls seated in the middle, the four teenagers snuggled tightly in the spacious backseat of the car, Billie's suggestion that someone ride in the front seat was summarily rejected by each of them. Minutes later, Billie dropped them at the main entrance and told them she would be back at nine o'clock to pick them up and drive them to the pizza parlor.

As Darrell and CJ held the rear doors open for Tanisha and Lori, Billie slowly pulled away from the curb and waved back at the couples. Tanisha exhaled. The drop off portion of the date had gone smoothly. She was really enjoying the new Billie.

The couples entered the building and walked the twenty steps to the main multi-purpose hall that served as the school's theatre and cafeteria. The lights were out and strobe lights sprinkled stars on the school's mascot, a purple pirate that served as the centerpiece in the multi-purpose hall. Once inside the building, Lori and CJ held hands and nuzzled. Following CJ's lead, Darrell reached for Tanisha's hand and she placed her fingers in his palm and discreetly rolled her eyes into the top of her head. His palms were sweaty. The girls gave the dance tickets to the chaperones at the door and the couples walked hand in hand into the dance. The disc jockey was playing *Rapture* by Blondie and teenage couples swayed to the beat.

Tanisha and Lori excused themselves to go into the bathroom. Tanisha's menstrual cycle had stopped the day before, but she still wore a sanitary napkin just in case. She went into a stall to use the bathroom as Lori reapplied her lip gloss. The bathroom was empty except for Tanisha and Lori.

"I'm so excited to be here. The decorations look so nice. I'm so glad they decided to do the under the sea theme. It looks cool. Don't you think, Tanisha?" Lori asked.

"Yeah, it looks nice." Tanisha was relieved that the sanitary pad was still dry.

"Darrell really likes you. I keep catching him staring at you." Lori applied more lip gloss to her already glossy lips.

Tanisha flushed the toilet and joined Lori at the sink to wash her hands. "Do you have any tic tacs?" Tanisha didn't want a tic tac for herself but wanted to be prepared to offer Darrell one in case he tried to kiss her. She'd gotten a quick whiff of his breath and thought it smelled like boiled eggs. She also thought she saw food hanging from his braces.

"Okay, what's up? You don't even look like you're into him." Lori stared at Tanisha in the mirror.

"Is it that obvious? He's nice enough, but I'm just not feeling him anymore," she groaned. "When we talk on the phone it's so lame! All he wants to do is talk about basketball and who's kissing who at school. We don't have any of the same classes, so we can't talk about school work. I'm beginning to wonder how he got elected student council president. He seems to have the IQ of a pretzel. And to make matters worse, his hands are sweaty and clammy!" Tanisha groaned.

Lori laughed. "Okay, that was funny. No one ever said he was a rocket scientist, but you have to admit that he's fine and he really likes you."

"He's cute, but those braces are beginning to bug me. And he has food stuck in them which is so gross and his breath is kicking! I want to offer him a tic tac!" Tanisha wrinkled her nose and made a face.

"Oh ick! I didn't notice that. You're cracking me up! Well, at least pretend to have a good time at the dance. I wish I had a tic tac or a mint for you. We'd better scoot before they get worried," Lori said.

Tanisha and Lori rejoined Darrell and CJ and decided to get some punch. The Turnabout committee had used three dimensional fish that the art students had created as the primary decoration. The fish were suspended at different heights from fish hooks connected to the ceiling tiles. Rubber fish floated in the red punch, a large rubber shark fin circled the bowl. A pirate figure hung on the rim of the punch bowl, a sword drawn as though he'd killed the shark and the fish were swimming in shark blood. The snacks were Pepperidge Farm goldfish and butter cookies shaped like fish. The centerpiece was a cake shaped like a dolphin. Tanisha had to admit that the committee had done a lot of work to transform the main hallway into an underwater adventure. She gulped down her punch and decided to adjust her attitude.

Darrell and Tanisha danced to Parliament's *Flashlight*.

As Tanisha danced to her favorite song, Darrell worked his pick-up lines on her.

"I was really glad when CJ told me that you wanted to go to the dance with me," Darrell said.

"Really? Why?" Tanisha asked.

"I really like you, Tanisha, and I want you to go with me," Darrell said confidently.

Tanisha had felt this question coming all week. Darrell had been calling her every day, and he'd been waiting by the gymnasium door so that he could see her before she went to pom pon practice on Tuesday and Thursday. Ironically, the more time she spent with Darrell, the less she liked him. Tanisha continued to dance pretending that she hadn't heard Darrell's question.

"You're supposed to say okay or something," Darrell explained.

"Oh, I'm sorry. Did you say something, Darrell?" she asked. "I spaced out for a minute. This is my favorite song."

"Tanisha, I asked you to go with me," Darrell repeated. He stopped dancing and stared at her.

"What does that mean exactly?" Tanisha asked. She took a deep breath and exhaled loudly.

"You know what that means." Darrell studied Tanisha's face.

"No, actually I don't. Define it for me," Tanisha said.

"It means we'll hang out and stuff," Darrell whispered in Tanisha's ear.

Tanisha didn't know what to do. Her Darrell crush had worn off, but she was curious to experience "going with" someone. She flashed her perfected closed mouth grin and spoke. "Sure, I'll go with you, Darrell." *Why did I say that?*

Darrell exhaled. "You had me worried. I've been spending all this time with you trying to get to know you and for a minute I thought you were going to say no. Cool. That's cool. I'll give you my locker combination. Come on, I'll show you where it is right now." Darrell grabbed her hand and led her to his locker.

Tanisha knew that Darrell was trying to get her to go to his locker so that he could kiss her. She'd heard from Lori and Maria that the kissing at the middle school dances occurred near the lockers. The locker corridor was dark and around the corner from the main dance area. Tanisha was surprised that the chaperones hadn't clued in to this make out row yet.

Darrell leaned Tanisha against his locker and placed her arms around his neck. He placed his arms around her waist. He spoke directly into her left ear and continued to talk in a low voice.

"Tanisha, I'm so glad you're my woman now. I've wanted to kiss you since seventh grade," Darrell purred.

Tanisha felt nothing and thought she might be sick to her stomach as Darrell breathed his sour breath in her face. She couldn't tell by the dim auxiliary lighting near the lockers, but she thought he had a piece of meat stuck in his braces. She wanted to run away as Darrell tilted his head to the left and leaned in to kiss her.

Tanisha closed her eyes, inhaled and braced herself for the boiled egg kiss. Darrell attacked her lips like they were polish sausages. His lips felt soft and moist but before she could decide if she enjoyed being kissed, Darrell was using his tongue as a battering ram to pry open her mouth, shoving his tongue down her throat and lathering saliva all over her lips. As Darrell's tongue moved around Tanisha's mouth, Tanisha found her tongue rubbing against Darrell's braces. All she could think about was the food stuck in his braces which repulsed her. She was afraid if he continued to kiss her, the thought of the food in his braces would trigger her gag reflex and she would vomit on him! Seconds later, Tanisha gently pushed Darrell away and wiped her mouth with the back of her hand. "We'd better get back to the party before we get caught by the teachers," Tanisha explained. She walked away without waiting for his response.

She was so disappointed. Her first kiss was nothing like she'd hoped. She'd read the Judy Blume novels <u>Are you There God? It's Me, Margaret</u> and <u>Deenie</u>. She had fantasized about being kissed for the first time, and this was nothing like she'd imagined. Tanisha dreamed that her heart would pitter patter and that she would want the kiss to last forever. Instead, she'd wanted the kiss to be over before it had started.

Darrell caught up to her and reached for her hand. Lori and CJ were having cookies and punch when Tanisha and Darrell walked up.

"Hey, girl! Where've you been?" Lori winked her eye twice confirming that she knew that Tanisha and Darrell had been kissing by the lockers. "Tanisha, will you come to the bathroom with me?" Lori asked.

"Sure. I have to go to the bathroom anyway," Tanisha replied dryly.

Once in the bathroom, Lori pressed Tanisha for details.

"Well, how was your first kiss?" Lori asked anxiously.

Tanisha took a deep breath and responded. "It was gross! His breath was harsh and his braces felt weird on my tongue. It was like he was licking an ice cream cone the way he ran his wet tongue all over my lips. And then I started thinking about the food in his braces and I almost got sick. So it only lasted about six seconds before I pushed him away and told him we'd better stop before we got caught."

"That's too bad. CJ is a great kisser. We're headed to the lockers right now. CJ asked me to hold his Tic Tacs in my purse. Take a few and offer one to Darrell." Lori popped a tic tac in her mouth.

Tanisha shook her head. "That won't be necessary. I am not kissing him again!" she announced loudly, emphasizing her point with her waving index finger.

"Well, just try to have fun since it's almost time for your mom to pick us up anyway," Lori pleaded.

They left the ladies room to rejoin their dates. The chaperones now sat comfortably in the folding chairs talking and laughing, some had removed their heels and rubbed their feet, seemingly oblivious to the teenagers who were disappearing into the locker area hand in hand. *Always & Forever* by Heatwave blared through the speakers. Tanisha groaned as Darrell walked toward her, reaching for her hand. "Let's dance," he suggested.

As they danced, she could smell his warm breath and thought she might gag. *I should have taken a Tic Tac from Lori.* She excused herself to go to the bathroom again and returned with two glasses of punch. *Maybe this punch will kill his bad breath.* As they sat on the cafeteria bench sipping their drinks, Tanisha's thoughts wandered to the roller skating rink and David Barton.

Chapter 18

Operation Fox Trot

Maria and Rashanda arrived at the skating rink promptly at seven o'clock. The crowd was smaller due to the Battle Creek Junior High Turnabout Dance, but some of the usual Friday night skaters were present.

Maria had arrived at Rashanda's house early and helped her pick out an outfit. She'd chosen a pair of jeans and told her to borrow a sweater from her younger sister Tiffany. Rashanda had protested, but Maria had insisted. "If the sweater is too small it will make you look shapely," Maria advised.

Once again Maria's fashion sense had been right. Rashanda's sweaters hung loosely around the bust area, but when she put on Tiffany's sweater, it made her size thirty inch chest appear much fuller.

As Rashanda's mom pulled into the skating rink parking lot, Maria nudged Rashanda in the side and whispered. "There's Todd's car." She pointed to a red Toyota Supra parked next to a black Corvette. Rashanda's heart skipped a beat as she braced herself to meet David Barton.

The girls grabbed their skates and paid their admission fee and entered the rink. They put their skates and jackets into a locker with Maria proudly stating. "We won't be using these tonight!" Maria waited five minutes to ensure that Rashanda's mom had driven away before she ran to the parking lot to let Todd know that she'd arrived.

Rashanda ran to the ladies room to freshen up. She gave herself the once over in the mirror and decided that she looked pretty good. Rashanda had begged her mom to let her wear her hair down, arguing that she was the only eighth grader who still wore her hair in more than one pony tail! Her mom had finally agreed to allow her to wear it down that evening and Maria had used a curling iron and styled it into a short mushroom style. At first, Rashanda thought she looked like Moe from the Three Stooges but she was so glad to be free from the ponytails that she didn't care. She slid her glasses off her nose and placed them in the eyeglass case that she'd thrown in her purse. Leaning closely into the mirror, her nose almost pressing against the glass, she reapplied her lip gloss and checked her braces to ensure that she didn't have food in them.

When she walked out of the restroom everything was a blur. She slanted her eyes intently, squinting horribly as she tried to discern where the main door was located. Without her glasses, the room was fuzzy, but she got her bearings and walked toward the front of the skating rink.

Maria and Todd were holding hands and Todd was tickling Maria as David Barton looked around the rink hoping to spot Tanisha.

When Maria spotted Rashanda, she waved her hand and motioned her toward them.

"David, here comes my friend now." Maria smiled widely in Rashanda's direction.

Friend? Singular? Doesn't she mean friends? Plural? He looked in the direction that Maria pointed and stared as Rashanda approached. His jaw dropped. His eyes quickly scanned the roller rink to see if there were any other girls walking toward them. Fortunately, Rashanda's vision was blurry and she couldn't see the obvious look of shock that registered on David's face.

"David, this is Rashanda. Rashanda, this is David Barton," Maria said, squeezing Todd's hand.

"Hello. It's nice to meet you," Rashanda smiled. She wasn't sure if she should shake his hand, so she fiddled with the strap of her purse.

"Hello, Rashanda. Same here," he smiled. "Todd, man, can I talk to you for a minute?" David didn't wait for a reply. He grabbed Todd's arm and pulled him toward the boys' bathroom.

"I thought you said that Maria always came with a group of girls. Where's everybody else?" David held on to Todd's shirt collar.

"Oh, there was some teeny bopper boy girl dance at their school tonight and her other friends went to that. What's the big deal?" Todd swatted David's hand from his shirt.

"Why didn't you tell me that?" David quizzed. *Tanisha must be at the dance with her boyfriend.*

"What difference does it make? Her friend Rashanda is here. Just have fun. I'm about to take Maria for a ride." Todd squeezed David's arm and walked out of the bathroom.

David was trapped. He knew that Todd and Maria would be gone for a couple of hours which meant that her friend Rashanda would be left to skate alone if David bolted. No, he couldn't leave her there by herself. He was too much of a gentleman for that. David rejoined the group.

"Have fun you two!" Maria waved backward as Todd pulled her to the door.

"So, Rashanda. Where are your skates?" David exhaled slowly.

"They're in the locker with our coats," Rashanda explained.

"You must be a pretty good skater to be able to skate with your skates in your locker," he teased. Rashanda looked at David with a blank expression. *Oh goodness! Tanisha would have cracked up and rattled off a witty comeback. It's going to be a long night.* "Tell you what. Why don't you get your skates and I'll rent some skates," David suggested.

David hadn't skated in two years. *I might as well get some exercise. I could kill Todd!* David walked to the skate rental booth.

ରୋ

Lori and CJ were making out near the lockers when the main hallway lights came on full blast. They quickly found Darrell and Tanisha and walked toward the main door to wait for Tanisha's mom.

Billie arrived fifteen minutes early and was waiting in the car when the couples came out of the school building. She hadn't wanted to disappoint Tanisha by being late.

"Hey, mom! We're all set." Tanisha was glad that her mother was waiting for them. It would make the evening end that much sooner.

Billie steered the car away from the curb and drove the five blocks to Sanfratello's Pizza. She checked with Tanisha again to ensure that she had enough money before driving away.

"Tanisha, your mom is cool," Darrell said as they walked into the restaurant.

"Yeah, she's okay," Tanisha agreed.

Their group was the first to arrive so they were seated in a booth located near the juke box. The girls ordered pizza and a pitcher of root beer while the boys studied the juke box song list.

Tanisha tried desperately to have a good time, but she was not enjoying Darrell's company. She was polite and witty, and allowed Darrell to put his arm around her shoulder after they finished their meal, but she was glad when shortly after ten o'clock Mrs. Perkins arrived to take them home.

Mrs. Perkins was a big woman, with a bigger personality. She had a heart of gold and was a surrogate mother to Tanisha. Mrs. Perkins was very comfortable in her skin and didn't apologize for her girth. Her favorite saying was: "Nobody wants a bone except a dog!" *I should ask Mrs. Perkins to help me with my black girls eat, white girls don't thesis.* Tanisha giggled to herself, smiled in Mrs. Perkins' direction and waved.

Darrell followed Tanisha's gaze and frowned. He spoke with a mouth full of pizza. "Whew! I'm surprised that big woman fit through the door!" Darrell laughed loudly. The pizza dough, cheese and meat rolled around in his mouth.

CJ threw Darrell a death stare and whispered. "That's Lori's mother, Darrell!"

"Oh, my fault. I've never met your mother, Lori, no offense," Darrell said.

Lori rolled her eyes at Darrell and held up one finger and shouted. "We'll be right out, Ma!" She turned her gaze to Darrell and continued. "You're an idiot, Darrell. Even if it wasn't my mother, what gives you the right to comment about someone's size?"

Darrell didn't know what to say. He looked at Tanisha for support but Tanisha just stared at him, raised both of her eyebrows and shook her head disapprovingly.

"It was just a joke. I didn't mean any harm. If I had known it was your mother," his voice trailed off.

As far as Tanisha was concerned that was strike two. His bad breath had been strike one.

The couples went outside where the April air was noticeably cooler. Tanisha draped her mother's pink shawl across her shoulders grateful that Billie had suggested that she bring it. They piled into the back of Mrs. Perkins' car for the ride home. As they climbed into the backseat, Darrell reached into his pocket and pulled out a pack of gum. He offered a slice to Tanisha, but she refused. *He's probably trying to freshen up his breath for another kiss. Too late for that! That ship has sailed!*

As they pulled away from the restaurant, Darrell rolled down the window and casually tossed his gum wrapper into the night air. Tanisha's jaw dropped from shock. *Strike three! If he is too ignorant not to litter, then I can't be bothered with him!* "I can't believe that you just did that," Tanisha said indignantly.

"Did what," Darrell asked. "I offered you a piece of gum. Did you change your mind?"

Tanisha stared at him dumbfounded. *He has no idea what I'm talking about. He must think that it's perfectly acceptable to litter. What a moron!*

As they pulled up to Darrell's house, Tanisha asked Mrs. Perkins if she could get out for a moment to use Darrell's bathroom quickly.

"We'll go through the side door to the garage," Darrell explained. He held the door open for Tanisha. As they walked toward the house, he leaned in and whispered, "That was smooth, Tanisha. I was going to tell you to say that you had to go to the bathroom. If we stand by the side door, she won't see us and I can kiss you again." Darrell grabbed Tanisha's hand and attempted to lead her to the side of his house.

Tanisha pulled her hand away forcefully. "You must be kidding," she said. "I didn't like the first kiss and I don't like you." Her voice was confident and firm. "You're a litter bug, you have the I.Q. of a potato chip, you're insensitive and your breath stinks. I quit you, so please don't ever call me again, Darrell!"

"What? You're kidding, right? Do you know how many girls would die to be my girlfriend?" Darrell's mouth hung open.

"Do you know how many girls you could kill with that bad breath of yours? And brush your braces after you eat, you have food in your teeth. It's disgusting! Good bye!" And with that, Tanisha marched proudly back to Mrs. Perkins' car smiling widely, not caring if her rotten tooth was displayed in her grin.

"What was that about? It looked like you were fighting!" Lori asked.

"I'll tell you later. Call me tonight." Tanisha settled in her seat for the short ride home.

Chapter 19

A New Leaf on the Same Tree

"How was the dance, Tanisha?" Billie Mae put down her magazine when Tanisha walked in.

"It was fine." Tanisha folded up the pink shawl and laid it across the sofa. "Here's your shawl."

"You can have it if you want. In fact, I can make one for you in a different color if you'd like. Better yet, I can teach you how to knit. Do you want me to teach you how to knit, Tanisha?" Billie's eyes were wide and she smiled broadly.

Tanisha stared at her curiously and shook her head. "No thanks. I can just borrow your shawl whenever I need it. And I don't really want to learn how to knit." Billie's behavior unnerved Tanisha. She was glad that Billie wasn't yelling at her, but she didn't completely trust her newfound niceness.

"So what did you do at the dance?" Billie asked. "Sit down and tell me all about it." Billie patted the cushion next to her on the sofa.

Tanisha paused and sat in the chair facing the sofa. "We danced and talked." Tanisha studied Billie's face. *What is she up to?*

"Were you warm enough in my shawl? I know it was pretty chilly when I dropped you off at the pizza parlor," Billie stated.

"It was fine. Actually, I'm really tired, and I need to call Lori before it gets too late. I left my lip gloss in her mom's car and I want to make sure that she finds it," Tanisha lied.

"Okay. Maybe you can tell me more about the dance in the morning," Billie said. There was a hint of disappointment in her voice. "I'm cooking breakfast in the morning. Would you rather have grits or biscuits or both?"

Tanisha stood up slowly. "It doesn't matter to me. I'll probably just have a bowl of cereal since I have to be at Save Mart at nine o'clock," Tanisha said confused. *Billie never cooks breakfast.*

"Do you need me to take you to work? I don't mind," Billie offered.

"I don't mind riding my bike. I'm used to it now, and I could use the exercise after all of the pizza that I ate. But thanks for the offer," Tanisha replied. *What is going on with her? What's with the niceness?*

"No problem. Goodnight," Billie said.

"Goodnight." Tanisha skipped up the stairs two at a time to call Lori. She hung her sundress in her closet and changed into her favorite rugby sleep shirt. She used the bathroom and brushed her teeth. Her menstrual flow had stopped completely. She called Lori and relayed the driveway dump to her friend.

"Wow! I am scared of you! It took a lot of guts to dump the most popular boy in eighth grade!" Lori said.

"I'd rather be by myself than attached to some insensitive dweeb," Tanisha explained. "He irked me all night. I can't believe that I kissed that creep. I wasted my first kiss on a creep! I'm such an idiot!" she groaned. She punched her pillow for effect. "Since the kiss lasted less than ten seconds, that doesn't count as a first kiss, right?" Tanisha pleaded.

"Well, technically, a first kiss is a first kiss. But we can say that the kiss has to last at least twenty seconds to really count," Lori said.

"Thank, Goodness! I'm not even going to tell the crew about that kiss. It was so gross I just want to forget that it ever happened," Tanisha exhaled. "I feel like I need to brush my teeth again."

"It must have been pretty bad. I won't tell a soul! We'll just pretend like it never happened!" Lori giggled.

"On a different note," Tanisha said. "My mom has been acting really nice lately," Tanisha whispered. "I don't know what's going on with her."

"Isn't that a good thing? I thought you hated your mother and wished that she were nicer," Lori replied.

"I do. I did. I don't hate her," she corrected. "But she's usually so mean that I don't like being around her," Tanisha clarified.

"Why are you whispering?" Lori asked softly. "Why am I whispering?"

Tanisha giggled. "Whenever someone whispers other people naturally whisper, it's weird. I'm whispering because Billie is downstairs. She totally waited up for me to come home. She was asking me all of these questions about the dance, and then she asked me what I wanted for breakfast in the morning!"

"I thought she never cooked," Lori said.

"She doesn't. But lately she's been cooking dinner. It's been so long since she's cooked breakfast that I didn't know what to say." Tanisha slowly opened her bedroom door and listened. She could hear her mom turning the pages of her magazine in the living room.

"Well, maybe she's turning over a new leaf. Maybe she's trying to make up for all of the meals that you cooked for her," Lori offered.

"Or maybe she's trying to poison me!" Tanisha said.

"You're so silly. She would not be trying to poison you," Lori scoffed.

"You can't be sure of that. Just in case, I'm not going to eat anything that she just cooks for me. If she makes my plate I'm going to switch with one of my brothers. I don't think she would try to poison them too," Tanisha continued. "If something happens to me, tell the police that I suspected that my mother was trying to poison me."

Lori laughed loudly. "Tanisha, she is not trying to poison you. She's your mother. You're not serious are you?"

"Promise me that you'll tell the police if I get some mysterious illness or die all of a sudden," Tanisha said. Her tone was serious.

"Okay, I promise. But now you're just acting paranoid," Lori said.

"She may not be planning to poison me, but I don't trust her. She's up to something," Tanisha said.

⚬~⚬

Downstairs, Billie flipped casually through the magazine. She barely glanced at the pictures and quickly skimmed the article titles. She desperately wanted to connect with Tanisha. Her therapist had told her that she had to make the first move in rebuilding the shattered relationship with Tanisha.

"The teenage years are difficult to navigate. They're especially challenging for mother-daughter relationships. Your situation is further compounded by your history of severe postpartum psychoses and the fact that you did not bond with Tanisha as an infant or toddler. So don't expect her to warm up to your attempts quickly. But you must try," he'd said.

Billie's hand shook. She wanted a cigarette. But she was trying to cut back and had already smoked her daily limit. She put a piece of Dentyne gum in her mouth instead and chewed. A car door slammed. She parted the draperies and waved as her neighbor walked around to open his wife's car door. Mr. Preston was always such the gentleman. He waved back as he helped his wife out of the car.

The house was quiet. Jack was still out with his friends, and Byron and Allen were spending the night at Jackie's house.

Billie missed Strongest. She settled into the sofa but changed her mind and decided to polish her albums. She grabbed the bottle of vinegar and her album polishing cloth and sat next to the stereo to wipe the dust from her record collection.

She put on Gladys Knight and the Pips' *Claudine* soundtrack and sang along. She missed being in a relationship whenever she heard ballads. She didn't outright miss Jackie, but she missed being in a marriage. She applied more vinegar to the cloth and wiped her forty fives too. The needle skipped. Billie carefully lifted the diamond needle and gently blew a small particle of dust away. After replacing the needle on the LP, Billie sat crossed leg on the floor and continued to nurture her records.

Chapter 20

Treasure Hunt

David and Rashanda skated one fox trot and one slow song together but mostly skated individually. Rashanda was a decent skater, and David's skating skills came back to him very quickly. He'd also spent a lot of time at the roller skating rink during his middle school years, and he remembered how excited he was the first time he asked a girl to skate. He wasn't a strong skater, but he'd successfully maneuvered both of them around the rink without falling. He smiled as he recalled that adolescent memory of just three years ago.

Thirsty from skating, David offered to buy Rashanda some refreshments. They sat across from each other to enjoy their snack.

"Rashanda, where do you go to school?" David asked unenthusiastically.

"I go to Battle Creek Junior High School. But we just call it the Creek," Rashanda said.

David paused, expecting her to ask where he attended school. He scrunched his eyebrows as she continued to nibble on her snack, seemingly oblivious to the follow-up question that was all but expected. He sighed. "Do you like school?" David's voice was flat.

"Yes." Rashanda needed to wear her glasses in order to skate. She removed her round rim glasses and cleaned them with the tip of her shirt.

"I met someone who goes to Battle Creek Junior High School or the Creek as you called it. I met her on the John & Judy ski trip.

I think her name is Tanisha," David said. "Do you know someone named Tanisha?" David didn't want to appear too frantic by recalling Tanisha's complete name to Rashanda.

"You must mean Tanisha Carlson. She's the only Tanisha at our school. I know Tanisha very well. We're in every class together except two. In fact, she told me to tell you hello. She's at the Spring Dance tonight," Rashanda rattled on.

David's eyebrows raised in unison. "She told you to tell me hello?" he asked excitedly. "How did she know that I would be here tonight?" He continued, sitting straight up on the bench.

"Maria mentioned that you would be here at lunch," Rashanda explained. She took a sip from her soda.

David decided to pump Rashanda for more information. "Tell her I said hello too. On the ski trip she mentioned that she was going to the dance with her boyfriend, what's his name again?"

"His name is Darrell Hunter, but he's not her boyfriend. Tanisha doesn't have a boyfriend. Darrell is the president of the student council, and he's on the basketball team. He's best friends with Lori's boyfriend, CJ, and Lori and Tanisha are like best friends so Tanisha asked him to go," she continued. "But today at lunch, Tanisha said she wasn't really that excited about going. She said that Darrell was getting on her nerves. I can't believe I'm telling you all of this." Rashanda carefully scraped the side of the nacho container with her last chip.

"That's okay. I don't mind." *So Tanisha really didn't have a boyfriend? Why did she tell me that she had a boyfriend then?*

"Were you with Tanisha when she met Byron Bird?" David asked carefully, trying not to appear too eager.

A mouth full of nachos, she shook her head up and down, waving a napkin that waited to wipe the cheese from her lip. Holding one finger in the air, she sipped her soda and swallowed hard. "I was," she said. "She met him at a John & Judy party a few months ago, and he asked for her phone number," she paused. "But he never called her. And then somehow Maria found out that he had a girlfriend and told Tanisha," she continued. David nodded his head and leaned in, surprised at Rashanda's candor, but glad that she had turned into chatty Cathy. Before he could phrase his next question, she continued, gesturing with her hands for emphasis. "Maria isn't really speaking to Tanisha and Lori right now because when Maria told Tanisha that Byron had a girlfriend, Tanisha told Maria that she was getting too skinny and that she should eat," she whispered. She looked over her shoulder and covered her mouth. "I probably shouldn't be telling you this," she said softly. "I don't want Maria to hear me talking about her."

Anxious to learn more, David leaned in. "Don't worry. I can see the door, and I'll tell you if I see them come in," he reassured. "This is interesting," he smiled. Returning his smile, Rashanda continued. "Tanisha also told Maria that Todd was controlling her and that he was too old for her to be dating. I don't know for sure," she said. "But somehow Lori got involved, and she agreed with Tanisha so Maria doesn't really talk to either one of them very much. It's like a middle school soap opera," Rashanda giggled. "And I'm caught in the middle because I'm friends with all of them," she finished, throwing her hands in the air.

"Todd can be kind of controlling," David agreed. "And don't worry, he's my friend, but I won't repeat any of this," he said seriously. "Does Tanisha still talk about Byron Bird?" David asked.

"Not really. She just said that on the ski trip his girlfriend got in her face and told her to leave her man alone or something like that. She hasn't talked about him at all this week. Why do you ask?" Rashanda picked at a nacho chip stuck in her braces.

David shrugged. "I saw Byron the other day at school, and he mentioned that he and Rebecca weren't working out," David offered. "He saw me talking to Tanisha on the ski trip and asked me if I knew how to get in touch with her," he finished.

"I could give you Tanisha's phone number to give to him!" Rashanda squealed. "Tanisha will be psyched. I'll write her number down for you." Rashanda reached in the small square pouch that was slung diagonally across her shoulder and pulled out a pen. She jotted Tanisha's number on a napkin.

David studied the number and slipped the napkin in his pocket. "Thanks, Rashanda. I'll give this to Byron next week at school." He glanced over Rashanda's shoulder. "Perfect timing. Todd and Maria are back," he pointed.

Todd and Maria approached arm in arm. Todd had Maria's lip stick smeared all across his face. "Hey, kids! How was the skating?" Todd asked. David handed Todd a napkin and motioned to his mouth.

"We had a good time!" David offered. He gathered the trash from their snack. "Rashanda let me tug her around the rink a few times and I got some much needed exercise," David said. "We've been skating for almost two solid hours, and I forgot what a good workout roller skating is. We just took a break to grab a snack," he explained as he stood up from the table clutching their trash. "Listen, I'm going to head out. It was nice to meet you, Maria. Take care, Rashanda!" David said cheerily, tossing their trash into the wastebasket as Todd walked into the bathroom.

Maria whispered to Rashanda. "Hey, girl! I saw you writing down your number for David! I'm scared of you. He's too fine!"

Rashanda looked innocently at Maria. "Oh, he didn't want my number. He wanted Tanisha's number to give to Byron Bird."

Maria's eyes opened as wide as saucers! *He wanted Tanisha's number? For Byron Bird? Wait until I call Rebecca!*

Maria Wesley wanted Tanisha Carlson out of her life, and she had been quietly working behind the scenes to destroy Tanisha's popularity since seventh grade. She smiled in her face and pretended to be her friend, but deep down Maria resented Tanisha. She resented Tanisha's self confidence and kindness and how she didn't seem to care what others thought about her. She resented how her own mother interacted with Tanisha and always held Tanisha up as an example of teenage perfection.

"Maria, why can't you be more like Tanisha?" Mrs. Wesley asked. "I always hear Tanisha talking about helping her mother around the house. Tanisha is active in the student council. Tanisha has a part-time job... Tanisha. Tanisha. Tanisha!"

When Tanisha met Mrs. Wesley for the first time, Maria immediately noticed how impressed her mom seemed with Tanisha. Maria thought that Tanisha was taking the goody goody role too far when she shared with Mrs. Wesley that she had to get home to start dinner for her brothers.

Maria was tired of the comparisons that her mother made with Tanisha so she'd secretly spread a rumor that Tanisha called Tracy Jones a buck tooth hillbilly. The rumor eventually got back to Tracy, and Tracy decided to get back at Tanisha by not inviting her to her party. Tracy never confronted Tanisha about the rumor; she just ostracized her from her birthday party which was far worse than any confrontation.

Although Tanisha was deeply hurt by not being invited to Tracy's birthday party, she put up a good front and pretended like it didn't bother her. Her nonchalant attitude annoyed Maria even more. If she had been left out of one of the biggest social events of the year, she would have begged and pleaded with the hostess for an invitation, perhaps calling the hostess' mother to garner an invite. She would have done something drastic to be there.

Although she feigned sympathy, she gloated over Tanisha's misfortune, publicly forcing her friend to discuss her exclusion in the cafeteria just days before the party. "I'm so sorry that Tracy didn't invite you to her party," Maria cooed. "Are you okay with that, Tanisha?" Maria secretly prayed for tears. She was shocked by Tanisha's cavalier response. "It's cool," Tanisha shrugged. "It seems like she invited everyone except me, so it feels kind of personal, but whatever," she continued. "She rolls her eyes at me in the hallway like she hates me, and since I didn't do anything to her I'm not losing any sleep over it. I think she might be mad that Darrell Hunter likes me," she finished. "She can have him as far as I'm concerned," she offered. "And if that's not why she treats me like dog poop, then I don't know what else it could be. I've never been anything but nice to her," she paused. "But Tracy and I don't have any classes together and I don't really know her that well. It's no big deal, really," Tanisha sighed.

Maria hung her skates on the hook in her garage and went to her room. She studied her reflection in the mirror. She was only five pounds away from her goal weight, and Todd hadn't mentioned anything about her being pudgy tonight. Thank goodness, because she'd hardly eaten anything all day and was feeling light headed. She'd almost fainted in P.E. because she barely had the energy to run the hundred meter sprint test.

As she gazed at herself in her bedroom's full length mirror, Maria peeled back her tee-shirt to reveal the hickeys on her chest. She and Todd had sat in his car all evening making out. She'd almost gotten caught by her mom the last time Todd left hickey marks on her neck so she'd told him to kiss her lower on her chest this time. They'd not gone past second base yet, but Todd was pressuring her to go to third base. After dropping off Rashanda, he dropped Maria off four doors away from her house in case her mom was looking out of the window expecting to see Rashanda's mom's car. She loved the feeling of living on the edge with Todd and not getting caught by her parents.

Maria put on her pajamas and decided to call her new friend Rebecca to find out what was going on with Byron Bird. She hadn't talked to Rebecca since the John & Judy ski trip but she already considered her a friend. She pulled her number from her purse and dialed. The phone rang three times and a teenage girl answered. Maria recognized Rebecca's voice.

"Hello, Rebecca? This is Maria." Maria sang into the phone in her cheerleader voice.

"Who is this?" Rebecca asked sternly.

"It's Maria. I met you on the ski trip. I'm Todd's girlfriend," Maria said.

"Oh. Hi." Rebecca's tone was flat and monotone.

Maria thought she could hear a hint of disappointment in Rebecca's voice.

"Did I catch you at a bad time?" Maria asked.

"That depends. What do you want?" Rebecca replied.

"I just called to chat. So where do you live?" Maria asked.

"I live in Lake Forest. Please tell me that you didn't call me to ask me that!" Rebecca demanded.

"No. I was just trying to make conversation," Maria replied softly.

"Marie, I'm busy doing my homework, and I'm waiting for a phone call. I really don't have time to talk with you right now," Rebecca exhaled loudly.

"It's Maria, not Marie. My name is Maria. How's Byron?" Maria asked.

"Well, whatever your name is. How should I know? I broke up with him last week. Listen, Marisa, I have to go." Rebecca hung up the phone.

Maria was stunned and stared at the receiver in her right hand. Rebecca hadn't offered to call her back or hadn't asked her to call her later. She'd simply hung up the phone.

Maria couldn't believe it. She and Rebecca had become fast friends on the ski trip. They'd acted like they'd known each other their entire lives. But now Rebecca treated her like a stranger. Tears flowed down Maria's cheeks as she ripped up the strip of paper with Rebecca's phone number on it and methodically tossed each shred into the wastebasket under her desk.

What have I done? Have I ruined my friendship with Tanisha for good? How can I fix it? She wiped her eyes with the back of her hand and studied her reflection closely in the mirror. She lifted up her pajama top and was shocked to see the outline of each of her rib bones protruding through her chest cavity. *Tanisha and Lori are right. I look like a skeleton.* She raced downstairs to the kitchen and made herself a peanut butter and jelly sandwich.

Chapter 21

The Sedated Tiger

The smell of fried chicken hung in the air. *Was Billie cooking dinner?* Tanisha tiptoed out of her bedroom and walked to the top of the stairs. She took another long breath. This time she smelled corn bread too. *What is going on?*

She walked back to her room and closed the door. She sat on the floor and crossed her legs. She needed to think. Her homework done, she picked up her pencil and twirled it slowly through her fingertips. *Billie has been acting strange. I'm going to list all of the things that I've noticed.* She grabbed her notebook and wrote.

- ✓ Cooking meals
- ✓ Paying bills on time
- ✓ Stopped practicing Buddhism and chanting
- ✓ Goes to Catholic mass now
- ✓ Stopped drinking beer
- ✓ Smokes a lot less and only smokes on porch now
- ✓ Makes her bed and cleans her room
- ✓ Hasn't been such a witch in weeks
- ✓ Got a new job at cable company

The fried chicken smelled delicious. Tanisha hoped that her brothers would get home soon. She hadn't ruled out her poison theory and would only eat food prepared by Billie in the presence of witnesses. On the back of her Billie list, she wrote the following:

Dear police, Please have the coroner check me for poisons, I think my mother may have poisoned me.

Signed,

Tanisha Carlson

She folded the note and tucked it in her pillowcase. *If I die suddenly, then she'll have to explain that one! I have to remember to tell Lori where I hid my just in case note for the police.*

She heard the front door open. It was her brother Byron. *Thank God he's home, at least now I can eat the chicken.*

A few days later, she shared her poison conspiracy theory with Jack. Her brother laughed and told her that she had an overactive imagination. But he reluctantly agreed to help her snoop around in Billie's room.

Tanisha wore yellow rubber gloves to hide any fingerprints.

"Tanisha, I don't' think you need to wear those gloves," Jack giggled.

"It won't hurt. Just look quickly and see what you find." Tanisha looked under the bed and felt between the mattresses.

"What exactly are we looking for, Tanisha?" Jack opened the top drawer and picked up a prescription bottle. "Tanisha, did you know that mom was taking lithium?"

Tanisha stood up and walked toward her brother. "Bingo! I knew it. She's trying to poison me!" Tanisha grabbed the brown prescription bottle and read the label. "Jack, what's lithium?"

"I'm not sure, but I think it's an anti-depressant medication. The only reason I know that is my friend Chris' mom takes it."

"Do you have any idea how long she's been taking it?" Tanisha handed the bottle back to Jack.

"Well, this prescription is only three weeks old," Jack said.

"Wow! I wonder if Dad knows that Billie's on lithium." Tanisha continued to look through Billie's drawers.

"Good question. Let's call him," Jack suggested. "Tanisha, what are you looking for now?"

"Poison. Who knows? I just thought since we're snooping we may as well be thorough. Go ahead and call Dad and I'll keep looking around to see what else she might be hiding." Tanisha carefully felt around the other drawers. *I do not trust her to make good decisions. She lacks good judgment! Remember the back rent? Keep snooping, Tanisha!* Tanisha's thoughts drifted to a Billie decision that would have destroyed her teenage existence.

A few months after their dad moved out, Jack and Tanisha discovered that Billie had stopped paying the rent. At the advice of one of her new Buddhist buddies, Billie was planning to move the family to a place in East Willow Heights, where the rent was one third the cost of what the family paid to live in Cedar Grove. Excited, Billie took Tanisha to see the unit that she was considering. As they drove into the complex, Tanisha's eyes filled with tears. Graffiti covered the sides of the concrete walls, barefoot children played in the parking lot, and a toddler rolled in the dirt filled plot where grass belonged, a bulging diaper her only article of clothing. Tanisha watched in dismay as a teenage girl scooped the baby from the dirt, placed her on her hip and continued her conversation. She shuttered as they side stepped a game of dice in front of the unit that was available for rent, the rental agent smiled warmly as they approached. Tanisha had to force herself to breathe. Once inside, Tanisha saw a large bug crawling along the wall. The carpets were stained and the unit had a musty odor. Faking a stomach ache, she stood silently in the open doorway as Billie toured the unit, listening to the profanity filled language of the children playing in the street. The tour complete, Billie rejoined Tanisha in the doorway. "What do you think, Tanisha?" she asked. The words stuck in her throat, Tanisha stared silently at her mother, too shocked and angry to speak or to cry. She simply shrugged. Billie tried to fill the ride home with comforting chatter. "The rental agent told me that they are moving out the bad element that lives there now, so if we decide to move in, those men won't be loitering in the front like they were today. She also told me that they're planning to paint the graffiti, and plant some grass," she continued. Tanisha stared at her mother's profile as she drove, chatting incessantly about the unit's potential. She turned her head away in disgust and stared out the window, wishing she could say what she was thinking. *You're an idiot, and you're too stupid to be responsible for four children!*

That night, Tanisha couldn't sleep. She tossed and turned, consumed with the thought that her family would be moving from one undesirable area to a worse area, a move that would place them in the worst school district in the city. In the morning, she walked to Vicky's house and shared her dilemma with her friend. When Vicky's mother, Mrs. Mildred returned from the store, Tanisha was sobbing uncontrollably. Tanisha was grateful that Vicky filled her mother in so that she wouldn't have to repeat the tale. Mrs. Mildred patted Tanisha's hand and gave her a hug. She took a deep breath and told her that as a single parent, her mother could qualify for a rent subsidy program which would allow Billie to remain in the family's Newberry East town home by paying reduced rent. She shared that she had a friend who worked at the government housing office and would place a call to get the paperwork sent quickly. She also said that she would pray for God to show favor on the Carlson family. She told Tanisha that she should also pray. Tanisha could see Vicky rolling her eyes at Mrs. Mildred. When her mother left the kitchen, Vicky whispered, "My mother is such a saint! She thinks that prayer is the answer to everything." Tanisha shrugged and walked home. *It certainly couldn't hurt.*

At bedtime that evening, she closed her door and knelt beside her new bed and prayed for the first time outside of church. She felt silly, and didn't know what to say. She looked around for a Bible, but couldn't find one in the house. Then she remembered that the main character in the book <u>Are You There God? It's Me, Margaret?</u> by Judy Blume would sometimes just talk to God and tell him what was going on in her life. Tanisha tried that. She told God that she didn't want to move, and that she was scared for her family's safety if they moved to East Willow Heights. She knelt in prayer each night and talked to God. She also checked the mailbox every day after school for the forms from the government housing office. On the third day, the documents arrived. Trembling, Tanisha presented the envelope to her mother immediately, already afraid that it might be too late.

"Mom, have you signed the lease for that unit in East Willow Heights yet?" Tanisha asked fearfully.

"Not yet," Billie replied. "I'm still thinking about it. Why?" Her mother asked.

"Well, I told Mrs. Mildred that we may have to move, and she suggested that you apply for this rent subsidy program," she said softly handing her mother the large envelope. "As a single parent, they'll help you pay part of your rent, and maybe we can stay in Cedar Grove," she paused. "I was talking to Vicky and started crying thinking about changing schools and leaving my friends. And Mrs. Mildred saw me crying and mentioned that the area has a really bad gang problem and they sometimes recruit boys whose fathers don't live at home," she finished quickly. "I don't think it would be a safe area for Byron and Allen to hang out. She also told me that a friend's son from church was shot in that subdivision," Tanisha lied. She braced herself for Billie's reaction, fearful that she would be angry that Tanisha discussed their family business with Mrs. Mildred.

Without a word, Billie pulled the paperwork from the envelope and studied it quickly. She admitted that she'd heard about a rent subsidy program but didn't know how to apply. She thanked Tanisha and asked her to get her a pen. She completed the paperwork and called the Cedar Grove rental office and explained her situation. Since the Carlson family had been tenants in good standing for several years, the property manager agreed to give her time for the federal rent subsidy application to be received so long as the back rent was paid by the end of the week. Next, Billie called Tanisha's grandfather and borrowed the money to pay the two months of back rent that she owed. Tanisha's heart raced as she watched her mother in action. Within a few weeks, the rent subsidy was approved, and the family's Cedar Grove lease was renewed. Tanisha would often turn her eyes to the sky and mouth, "Thank you, God" throughout the day. She now relished her Cedar Grove dwelling in a way that she never thought possible.

She stopped searching through Billie's drawer and snapped out of her daydream when she heard her brother talking to their dad on the phone.

"Hey, Dad! How was your day? Oh that's good. Listen, Tanisha was looking in Mom's drawer for some stockings and found a bottle of Lithium pills. Do you know why mom is taking lithium?"

Tanisha gave Jack the thumbs up. She hadn't thought about a reason for why they'd been looking through Billie's drawers.

"Oh. She's taking lithium?" Jackie inhaled, deeply. *He's sucking on a cigarette.*

"Uh, huh. I was just wondering if you knew anything about that," Jack replied.

Tanisha pressed her face against Jack's cheek to hear. There was a long pause.

"She hasn't said anything to you about it before?" Jackie asked.

"Nope. And Tanisha and I are just trying to make sure that she's alright," Jack explained.

"I see. That explains why she has been acting nicer to me lately, but I thought she was buttering me up to ask for more money. But how has she been acting with you kids?" Jackie took another pull from his cigarette.

"Great. You know that she started a new job, and she's been cooking dinner. She's stopped chanting and going to Buddhist meetings and now she goes to mass on Sundays and takes Byron and Allen. She's been acting normal," Jack said.

"I see." There was another long pause. Jackie took a deep, guttural breath. "Well, your mom has some mental issues and she should be taking medication all the time. But sometimes, she thinks she's better and stops taking her pills. This has been going on for years," Jackie explained.

Tanisha's eyes bugged when her dad said the words mental issues. "Mental issues? What kind of mental issues, Dad?" she asked.

"Is that Tanisha? I didn't know you were on the phone too. How you doing, Booger?" Jackie asked.

As long as she could remember, her dad had called her Booger. And now that she was a teenager, he still called her Booger. He always claimed that he didn't remember why he gave her the nickname Booger, but Tanisha got queasy thinking of possible reasons why her dad would nickname her after nose mucus.

"I'm fine, Dad. What kind of mental issues does Billie, I mean Mom, have?" Tanisha's nose crinkled when she said mental issues.

"Well, it's a long story. I'll tell you about it one day in person. But she's okay as long as she takes her medication. I thought she'd told you about this when I moved out. We talked about it, and she told me that she was going to tell you," he said. "I bet she's been off her medication for a long time. That's probably when she started doing that Buddhist stuff and quit her job. This is the same thing that happened the last time she stopped taking her medication. She turns her whole life upside down and everyone in her life goes on a roller coaster ride." Jackie took another pull from his cigarette. "Well, the good thing is that it sounds like she's back on her medication. Now don't say anything to her, just wait for her to tell you, but I'll try to tell you more this weekend when I see you. Do Byron and Allen know anything about the medicine?" Jackie asked.

"No, dad. Tanisha just found it accidentally and brought it to me to see if I knew what it was," Jack said.

"Good. They're too young to understand so just don't say anything to them." Jackie coughed into the phone.

Jack and Tanisha confirmed their weekend plans with their dad before hanging up the phone. They stared at each other. Jack spoke first.

"Wow! I had no idea. That explains a lot," Jack said.

"Like what? That explains what?" Tanisha asked angrily. She closed the drawers and peeled off her rubber gloves.

"No wonder she's been so moody sometimes. I thought she was going through menopause or something, but she just wasn't taking her medication," Jack said. He carefully placed the medicine back in Billie's drawer.

"She's not going through menopause. She's only thirty-six years old, you moron! Billie is still young enough to have children. Her tubes are tied, but if they weren't, she could still get pregnant. Most women don't start menopause until their late forties or early fifties." Tanisha exhaled loudly and continued. "Well, to me that's no excuse for anything. If she knew that she should have been taking medication to function normally, then it was irresponsible for her not to take it. She's an idiot!"

"Tanisha!" Jack scolded. "I think we need to understand why she takes the medicine before we jump to any conclusions and judge her. Give her a break, sis. You're not being fair," Jack said.

"Not being fair? It wasn't fair of her not to take medicine that she knows she needs to take every day!" Tanisha barked. "Give **her** a break? She needs to give **me** a break! I hate her guts!" Tanisha stomped to her room and slammed the door.

She leaned into the door and slid to the floor as the tears rolled down her cheeks. Tanisha had been angry and indifferent toward her mother for so long that the anger had become like a security blanket, shielding her from her mother. She crawled to her bed and climbed in, placing the comforter over her head, the thoughts racing quickly each battling for center stage. *So she's been on and off medication for years and she's back on it now? That explains why she's been nicer. She wasn't trying to poison me. Why didn't she tell us like Dad asked her to? What kind of mental illness does she have? Are there different kinds? So all of a sudden, she decides to take her mental medication, and now I'm supposed to be her new best friend? What if she decides to stop taking it again? Then what? I don't trust her! She is such an idiot! Am I supposed to feel sorry for her? If she knew she should be on medication, why wasn't she taking it? What will my friends think when they find out that she has a mental illness? God, why did you give me her as a mother? Can I pray this away?*

Consumed with anger and confusion, Tanisha buried her head in her pillow to muffle the uncontrollable sobs, biting her teeth into her pillowcase.

Chapter 22

Thriller

One of the perks of Billie's new job at the cable company was free cable installation and a free basic cable package for one year. So far, Maria was the only friend in Tanisha's group with cable. Tanisha was excited to finally have something that Maria had.

Billie was still trying to establish a closer relationship with Tanisha. She still had not shared her mental illness with her children, but she was taking her prescribed medication regularly. She was glad that Tanisha was excited about the cable and encouraged Tanisha to have a video party.

Billie bought party invitations that she helped Tanisha complete. Tanisha invited all of the friends from her slumber party: Lori, Rashanda, Grace, Justine and Maria. At first, she'd planned to exclude Maria, but Lori convinced her to invite Maria since she had been going out of her way to rejoin the group. Maria had been speaking to Tanisha at school and had called her a few times with questions about their algebra homework. They'd even done the fox trot together at the skating rink when Todd was out of town with his parents. She and Maria were cordial, but Tanisha still didn't trust her and held her at arms length.

All of her guests arrived promptly at six thirty to watch the Michael Jackson *Thriller* video marathon on MTV. The *Thriller* video was the only video being shown all night until midnight on MTV. Billie purchased chips and soda and set the snacks out on a card table in the living room. Once the girls arrived, Billie asked the girls if they would prefer Aurelio's or Sanfratello's pizza. Hands down the girls chose Aurelio's pizza, so she placed the order and left to pick up the food.

"Tanisha, your mom is really cool," Rashanda offered.

"Thanks. She has her moments," she replied.

Tanisha had not shared with any of her friends that her mother was taking anti-depressant medication. She was still confused and ashamed about her mother's mental illness. *If they find out that Billie is crazy, will they think that I'm crazy too?*

Billie returned with the pizza and retired to her room to read. The girls danced and sang along with the *Thriller* video trying desperately to mimic the intricate choreography.

After the girls watched their fourth video, they flopped on the sofa to take a break. Tanisha decided to toss out some of the paper plates while the other girls rested. Maria quietly followed Tanisha into the kitchen.

Tanisha was startled when she turned around to see Maria staring at her. Maria spoke first. "Tanisha, I just wanted to say that I'm sorry for treating you so poorly on the John & Judy ski trip. I don't know what got into me," Maria continued as Tanisha stared at her, stunned at the sincerity in her voice. "I barely know Rebecca, and I totally dismissed you like you were a stranger. I know my apology is long overdue since the trip was several weeks ago, but I'm really sorry." Her voice cracked as though she might cry. "I really miss your friendship," Maria sobbed.

"Don't cry, Maria. It's cool. I know sometimes when you meet new friends you want to throw out your old friends. I appreciate the apology," Tanisha said.

Maria wiped at her eyes. "Also, I know you and Lori were just trying to look out for me by noticing that I was getting too skinny.

And you were right. I'm not trying to lose any more weight! In fact, I'm trying to gain back some," she shared.

"Maria, you look great, and I noticed that you ate five or six pizza squares and I didn't see you running to the bathroom with a spoon!" The girls laughed at her bulimia reference before Tanisha continued. "No, but seriously, we were just worried about you, that's all. Todd should like you for who you are. If you want to change for yourself, then that's one thing, but you shouldn't let some knucklehead boy tell you what you should look like!" Tanisha searched the kitchen for a box of tissue but settled on a paper towel and handed it to Maria to wipe her face. "Remember, black girls eat, white girls don't."

"You are so right." Maria blew her nose into the paper towel. "Todd's a really good guy, and I think he was just teasing me, and I took his teasing about my weight too seriously," Maria defended. "My parents said I can date when I'm fifteen, so next year Todd and I won't have to sneak around. I know you and Lori don't like Todd, but I really like him and I want you guys to try to get to know him."

Tanisha smiled at her friend. "Deal. I haven't really had a chance to get to know him so I guess I judged him too quickly. But how can we get to know him when you disappear in his car as soon as we get to the skating rink? Maybe next Friday when we go to the rink you can make him hang out with us for a while and we can see what he's like. But even if we don't like him, I won't dis' him, at least not around you."

"Fair enough. And I'll make him rent some skates so we can skate next Friday. By the way, if you're still interested, Rebecca and Byron Bird broke up a few weeks ago, and he's been trying to reach you. I know that David Barton got your number from Rashanda to give to him."

"Yeah, Rashanda told me. But Byron hasn't called yet, and I'm not holding my breath," Tanisha exhaled.

"I'm sure he'll call, but if he doesn't, it's his loss!" Maria blew loudly into the paper towel. "Tanisha, I'm glad we're cool again."

"I'm glad we're cool, too!" Tanisha said. "Let me get you a tissue before that paper towel cuts your nose."

Maria extended both of her arms and Tanisha met her with a hug before rejoining the party.

Rashanda was the keeper of the cable box remote control and had been channel surfing in between the MTV marathon. She stopped as the *Golden Girls'* theme song played and started singing along. The other girls chimed in:

"Thank you for being a friend, Traveled down the road and back again, Your heart is true. You're a pal and a confidante, And if you threw a party, and invited everyone you knew you would see the biggest gift would be from me and the card attached would say thank you for being a friend."

"I love that *Golden Girls'* theme song," Tanisha shared.

Rashanda clicked back to MTV just in time for the start of the next *Thriller* video.

By nine o'clock the girls had overdosed on MTV and agreed to call it a night. Lori, Rashanda, Justine and Grace rode home with Rashanda's mom. Maria's mom had promised to take Maria's brother Neal for an ice cream sundae. Maria invited Tanisha to come along.

Mrs. Wesley pulled in front of Tanisha's house in her new Toyota Celica with black leather interior. Maria's younger brother Neal rode in the front seat with Mrs. Wesley so Tanisha and Maria climbed into the back seat of the shiny black sports car. As Mrs. Wesley slowly backed the car out of the parking spot, Tanisha noticed that she struggled to turn the steering wheel of the tiny car.

"Maria, why is the steering wheel so hard for your mom to turn?" Tanisha whispered.

"Oh, my mom special ordered a manual steering wheel to help keep her bicep muscles toned," Maria explained loudly. "The Toyota dealer told her that true sports cars have tight steering wheels. My dad hates driving this car and says my mom was stupid to special order manual steering when power steering is standard nowadays," Maria said loudly.

"Maria, I heard you. And you know I don't like you using the word stupid," she scolded. "It's my car, and I got exactly what I wanted," Mrs. Wesley winked at Tanisha in the rearview mirror.

Tanisha had never seen anyone drive a car with a manual steering wheel and was impressed at how well Mrs. Wesley maneuvered the vehicle. Tanisha studied Mrs. Wesley's mannerisms as she drove, noticing how she drummed her slim fingers along the leather steering wheel column and playfully tickled Neal at every stop light. Maria grimaced as her mom sang along with the radio while Tanisha relished the sound of her soft alto voice. She inhaled deeply and smelled the Opium cologne that Mrs. Wesley always wore. Tanisha called it her "signature scent." Tanisha had missed that scent, and had missed spending time with Maria and Mrs. Wesley. *I wish my mother had a signature scent.*

Tanisha ordered a scoop of butter pecan ice cream on a plain cone and Maria ordered a mint chocolate chip sundae. Mrs. Wesley ordered black walnut on a plain cone and Neal ordered a banana split. They ate the ice cream in the chilly ice cream parlor before climbing back into the warm car.

Tanisha was glad that she and Maria were friends again because she really enjoyed spending time in Mrs. Wesley's presence. She was amazed at how often Mrs. Wesley showered Maria with compliments and often said things like, "I just want you to be happy, Maria. If you're happy, then I'm happy." Tanisha envied the mother-daughter relationship that Maria had with her mom and longed for a mom like

Mrs. Wesley. As Mrs. Wesley pulled into the Cedar Grove complex, Tanisha thanked her again for the ice cream treat.

Mrs. Wesley got out of the car so that Tanisha could push the front seat up and exit from the driver's side. She reached for Tanisha's hand and pulled Tanisha into her arms for a hug. "It was a pleasure, Tanisha. I'm glad Maria invited you because I've missed seeing you around the house. Come and visit soon."

"I will. Thanks again, Mrs. Wesley." Tanisha's eyes misted. She walked toward her front door. As she stared at the dark green cedar siding covering the Carlson family's townhouse, Tanisha exhaled deeply. She admired the lush green lawns of the modest townhouses and the flower beds that graced most of the window sills. She tilted her head to the sky and mouthed, "Thank you, God." She was also grateful that Billie was still being nice. She wasn't as nice as Mrs. Wesley, but she was nicer than she'd been in a long time.

As she walked up the three steps of the front stoop and inserted her key to unlock the door, she realized that things didn't have to be as good as they were right at that very moment. She turned around to wave again and smiled widely without concern for her decayed front tooth. Mrs. Wesley smiled and waved back, and Tanisha thought for a moment about the friends that she'd made at Battle Creek Junior High. She was glad that at least she had made friends with a good group of girls. They weren't perfect, but they were caring, accepting and forgiving and they looked out for each other.

When Tanisha entered the small foyer, she saw that her brother Byron was home. During her *Thriller* video party, he and Allen had gone bowling with a neighbor's family. She noticed that the card table had been removed and the party mess cleaned up. She smiled again. *Wow! Mom is really trying hard! I could get used to this.*

Byron was watching a soccer game on the Spanish speaking channel. An avid sports fanatic, Byron didn't speak Spanish. Tanisha wondered how he understood what was going on. She smiled when she heard Allen snoring softly in the corner.

"Hey, Byron! You're still up?" Tanisha stretched her arms to the ceiling and yawned.

"Yeah. I'm watching this soccer game," Byron yawned, too. "Oh yeah, I was upstairs and your phone was ringing about an hour ago, so I answered it. It was a boy. He didn't leave his name, he just said that he'd call you back."

To Be Continued...

About JC Conrad-Ellis

A native Chicagoan, the author is a graduate of Northwestern University and Loyola University. JC currently lives in Hartland, Wisconsin with her husband and their three children. This is her first novel.

Go to www.boysbeautyandbetrayal.com for more information about the author, the characters and the books.

Coming Soon:
CAMP COLORBLIND – Part 2 in the Tanisha Carlson Series.

.

Printed in the United States
129332LV00004B/119/P